·LYSBET·

By the Same Authors:

THE FIVE GOLD SOVEREIGNS
THE CRIMSON SHAWL

Lysbet

A STORY OF OLD NEW YORK

by

Florence Choate

and

Elizabeth Curtis

WITH ILLUSTRATIONS
BY THE AUTHORS

PHILADELPHIA

J. B. Lippincott Company

NEW YORK

Contents

CHAPTER		PAGE
1	LYSBET SAILS	3
2	NIEW AMSTERDAM	17
3	LYSBET SETTLES IN	33
4	SUUSJE	45
5	SAINT NICHOLAS' EVE	57
6	SECRETS	70
7	WINTHROP'S VISIT	85
8	THE STUYVESANTS' HOUSEWARMING	100
9	JUDITH	116
10	UNEXPECTED MEETINGS	131
11	NICK BAYARD'S PEN-KNIFE	141
12	GERTJE	153
13	SCHOOLMASTER'S WEDDING	166
14	HANS AND JORIS	181
15	NIEW AMSTERDAM FALLS	193
16	LYSBET SAILS AGAIN	210

Authors' Note

In the spirit of the age, the author has used the contemporary—and variable—spelling of proper nouns as drawn from old documents.

·LYSBET·

CHAPTER ONE

Lysbet Sails

❦

LYSBET WENT LAST AS WAS BECOMING HER AGE AND CIR-
cumstance. She might have taken this cliff in a few leaps,
sure as a young mountain goat, but all of them were held
back by the Lord General who was slowed up by his
pegged leg. Heading the company he thrust its point
between the stones, feeling for a firm foundation. The
path down to the banks of the Hudson was rough as well
as steep.

Cornelis Van Ruyven, Secretary of the Province, came
next with high officials of Niew Amsterdam; its Captain, Martin Cregier, with the Burgher Guard; then
Dutch soldiers and the bound hostages, twelve sullen
Indians. The interpreter, Mevrouw Kerstedt, followed
them and behind her came Domine Megapolensis; then
Lysbet.

The river was below them and above was the small
settlement of Wiltwyck with its blockhouse and high
palisade. It had seen great tribulation in a long-drawn-
out Indian war. This had now come to an end through
a swift campaign by General Stuyvesant and his well

equipped force. The redskins, with a few guns illicitly traded to them by the whites and their own primitive weapons, could not hold out long.

The signing of the treaty had been the occasion of much ceremony and display, with the sachems of seven neighboring tribes gathered to witness it. His excellency, Petrus Stuyvesant, Director of Niew Netherland as well as Niew Amsterdam, General of their military forces, signed for the Dutch; then two of his Burgomasters, then Arendt Van Corlaer, Secretary of the powerful patroonship of the Van Rensselaers.

Four sachems of the defeated Esopus tribe made their marks. They promised to sell land to the whites and keep their own land at a distance, to repay heavily in corn for the ransoms they had wrung from prisoners, to kill or pillage no more. "This done and concluded," the treaty ended, "at the settlement at the Esopus, under the blue sky."

There were fewer in the settlement than there had been two years before, but now Director promised to give land on easy terms and build it up again.

The official barge of the Province lay in the channel. General Stuyvesant stepped into one of its landing boats. Settling himself in the bow he wiped his face with a fine, lace-trimmed handkerchief for he had made a greater effort than he had cared to show. Secretary Van Ruyven and the two Burgomasters got in after him the boat listing perceptibly.

The hostages went in a second boat, the soldiers handling them roughly. These men had been the ring-leaders so should be sent to Curaçao, a Dutch island in the West Indies, and be sold as slaves. "Silver Peg" as they called the Director, from silver nails on his pegged leg, had reached the end of his usual patience with the redskins.

Mevrouw Kerstedt, with Lysbet and some of the Guard, went next. When they reached the barge one of the sailors leaned over the side and pulled Lysbet up the ladder. "What have we here?" he asked, grinning. "If my eyes see me straight, no beauty."

He was no beauty himself, thought Lysbet, but being a man could not be sauced like Dirck and Jon Goosen. These two worthys were up on the cliff with a crowd of Indians, soldiers and settlers, watching them off. Older than she and hateful besides, they had plagued her cruelly. She was fighting them in a fury when the Domine had seen her first.

Tired by her duties as interpreter, Mevrouw Kerstedt went below but Lysbet, seeming to be forgotten, sat herself on a coil of rope, nursing her thumb. In the fight with the Goosens it had got disjointed, and though Domine had yanked it back, it was still sore and the sailor had not helped it.

Lysbet was a tall child of about twelve and showed neglect. Her face with its gaunt cheekbones and intense blue eyes looked too old for the rest of her. A careless hand had hacked her sun-bleached hair; her dress was outgrown and faded.

They had embarked on a center deck but there were higher decks, fore and aft. A few of the company climbed to the fore deck but most of them stayed below.

The Lord General waved aside a bench and stood at the rail as the anchor was drawn and the sails lifted. The tide was strong and without much wind the barge was off, sliding down the river. His stern face had relaxed in pleasant anticipation of this water trip. He acknowledged a cheer and gunshot from the shore.

Philip Schuyler, a young trader and Rensselaerswyck's vice-director, stood at his elbow. He wished to found a new settlement near Wiltwyck now that peace had been made and this seemed the time to talk of it.

They were tacking in order to catch all the wind there was, and at this unfortunate moment when the deck stood at an angle, the General started for his bench. His spiked leg slipped, he lost his balance. Philip Schuyler, with others, rushed forward in alarm but Lysbet, nearer to him, was there before them. Her klump braced the point and stopped it short. "Hold on t' me," she yelled shrilly.

The General caught himself then looked at her with his keen Dutch eyes. "Our friend Aesop tells us a mouse may save a lion, but can I ask, jonge juffrouw, who are you?"

Ashamed at being so forward Lysbet evaded his
glance. "Lysbet," she faltered, "but the men was there. If
I ha' but looked I would no ha' lept."

Philip Schuyler laughed. "Leaped before she looked.
Most effective that time."

The Lord General smiled grimly. "The child is a bag of bones."

"It shows what those poor folk have undergone," said Secretary Van Ruyven. Then he added hastily, "But seat yourself, Excellency. We tack again!"

"I have not finished," said his Excellency, bracing himself." Tell me, child, did you lose your parents in this trouble?"

"No," said Lysbet, looking to the ground, "they was not killed then."

His Excellency glared about him. "Then why is she here? We do not want to separate families. Niew Amsterdam has its own to care for."

Lysbet hastened to explain. "Domine brought me. He says Goosens was worse to me than naked savages were. I won't be no charge for I can work. He aims to bind me out."

"Bind her out! Jehoshaphat!" His Excellency exploded. "Bind her out to eat and get some fat on her bones, rather." Then he spoke more moderately. "It is 'your Honor' when you address me, child. Do not forget it."

"Yes-yes, your Honor." Lysbet retired to her corner.

The river turned, broadened, then narrowed again. Hills and forest bound it in but there was no sign of human life or habitation. Only the wilderness stretching on the east to the English settlements, on the west to distances unknown.

Lysbet looked to the east and then to the river. Was it on this that the Mohawks had brought her? It was one like this, broad and with a strong current. She remembered the sweep of the paddles as they had fought against it, the muscular backs of the braves, the occasional guttural word, her own utter despair.

Back of that had been her father's cry, "Elizabeth, run!" Her mother had taken her hand and they had run. Her mother had fallen and as she lay had cried, "Elizabeth, run!" She would not run and then a Mohawk had caught her.

Swinging her over his shoulder they had started that ceaseless tramp, tramp, tramp, leaving a burning house behind them. It was a narrow trail and the party had walked in single file. The leader had carried her father's gun. Bloody scalps were hanging at his belt. Twigs had caught in her hair and she had shrieked in fear of having her own scalp torn off. How long they had walked she could not remember, but they had slept in the forest many nights.

When they reached their village beyond Rensselaerswyck the Indians had not been unkind. One of the squaws had mothered her more or less. The children had called her "Swannekin," laughing at her white skin and yellow hair. As time passed and she learned their ways, they had accepted her. She had lived and played with them, struck out with them when older boys threw them in the lake. Like them all she learned to swim like a fish, to fight for her rights, to stand pain without crying.

There had been one child," Little Beaver" whom she had loved. On a tragic day they had wandered off together and stirred up a nest of rattlers. He had been stung and before they could stumble back to the village the poison had gone through his body.

Lysbet remembered her grief, the lamentations of the women, the silence of the father. Little Beaver was buried with wampum and food to serve him on his journey to the other world, his bowl and spoon, his bow and arrows.

In the freedom of the spring, summer and autumn she had been content; as the memory of her home and parents faded, even happy. But she had hated the winters with all huddled into a close shelter with a frozen world outside. She had hated the killing of the animals, the curing and packing of the evil smelling furs. These were taken to the trading post at Rennselaerswyck or to the Company's post at Fort Orange.

As to who the "Company" was even the braves had been hazy. "Silver Peg" was their chief. Like all the "Swannekins" they were greedy for beaver skins. These were sent to Niew Amsterdam, and then across the sea, there to be traded for "heap wampum."

The braves would bring back from Rensselaerswyck and Fort Orange "heap wampum" and tools used by the Swannekins, the firewater, which led to a night of terror, occasionally the forbidden firearms. These were used against their hereditary enemies, the northern Algonquins, or the Hurons, allied with the French beyond the lakes. They would bring back from the warpath scalps of coarse black hair, and prisoners to ransom or torture.

Hating this more than all, Lysbet would run and hide and the children, all but Little Beaver, jeered at her squeamishness.

One of the braves finally let out that they had a captive white child. Arendt Van Corlaer, highly trusted by the Mohawks, had ridden miles through forest trails, to ransom her. There had been sharp trading, for the squaw wished to keep her. She would soon be strong enough to work in the planting fields and with the furs and beads.

By the handing over of much wampum and promise of favor, Arendt had driven his bargain and ridden off with Lysbet clinging on behind him. Speaking in the Indian tongue he had asked if she remembered her father's name, her own, where they had lived, how old she had been when the Mohawks had got her.

The only name she remembered was Elizabeth. She had been five winters with the Mohawks. They must have lived far distant for first they had walked, then taken canoes.

She must have come from one of the English settlements, Arendt told her. The Mohawks, friendly with the Dutch, frequently made distant forays. In view of that it was useless to try to find her people. He would put her with Dutch people, like himself, and she must learn their ways. She must forget savage ways for by birth she was a Christian, not a heathen.

He put her with the Goosens, a family who were moving from Rensselaerswyck to Wiltwyck. As they had only sons they thought a girl might be useful. There were fields to clear and a house to build; there was planting, weeding and reaping; hungry mouths to feed, washing and scrubbing. Lysbet and Vrouw Goosen worked together, for this pioneer life meant work. Lysbet was too young for it.

They had been at Wiltwyck for two years when the Esopus tribe went off like a spark in dry timber. Word came from Niew Amsterdam that the scattered settlers must live within a stockade, with their fields outside. There was the building of a new home, two more years of work and fear, the final terror when the savages gathered outside the village, sending blazing arrows to fire the straw roofs.

One of the settlers had gone to Niew Amsterdam for help. The Lord General had come with troops and settled the matter. And now she herself was going there. Domine Megapolensis and Arendt Van Corlaer had said the Goosens were not fit to keep her.

She thought of Little Beaver. He was not like those who had threatened them. He was gentle and would not harm the littlest thing. She knew now that he had died to save her. She thought of the wampum and food, the bowl and spoon, his tiny bow and arrow. If he had lived would he have grown to be like the others? She could not think so.

Domine Megapolensis had been talking to Burgomaster Olif Van Cortlandt, but looking at Lysbet. Her lonely appearance troubled him. The poor child had been through so much and more might come. He hoped to find her a home with his daughter, Mevrouw Van Ruyven, but he did not know. He had only known that she should not be left with the Goosens. Ignorant to begin with, they had coarsened under the rigors of pioneer life.

The child could know little to fit her to live with nice people and the readjustment would be hard. Could he help her now in a simple way that she might understand? She looked bright and was quick in going to the Director's aid. Explaining his purpose he left the Burgomaster and took a seat.

"Lysbet," he called, "come to me. I wish to talk to you."

Lysbet came timidly. He looked so sober in his black dress and bands, but as she sat herself beside him she saw that he was smiling at her, not frowning like the Director.

"Well, Lysbet, you are to live in Niew Amsterdam," he said. "Tell me, what do you know of Niew Amsterdam?"

"It be a splendid place," said Lysbet, "with a fort not sticks but stone, a kerk, a mill that goes wi'wind, many fine houses. Ensign Smit, wi'the soldiers, told me. I know not if he were boastful, your Honor."

"Perhaps a little over-boastful," said the Domine. "We do not call it splendid, but pleasant and comfortable. Old Amsterdam is the city of splendor."

"He told me of that, too," said Lysbet, "but then I did no' believe him. Those were foolish tales—"

The Domine laughed. "I do not know what he told you, but you must believe me now. I have seen Amsterdam with my own eyes many times, and tell you the truth."

Choosing his words carefully he told her of the lands beyond the sea, of their people, of the towns and cities, the least of which would dwarf Niew Amsterdam. He told her of the seven Provinces of the Netherlands, called Patria by those who loved it, of Holland, the greatest of the seven, with its important city of Amsterdam.

The Netherlands was a Republic, he said, for it had no king like their neighbors but was ruled by a number of men, selected from the seven Provinces, called their High Mightinesses; the States General.

He had been right as to the child's intelligence. Her face intent, she had been drinking in his words. "Now, Lysbet, we have gone as far as this. But is there some question that you would care to ask?"

Lysbet spoke eagerly, "I thought it were his Honor—

I thought it were the Company. All the talk is of them—"

The Domine wondered how he could explain this, yet not muddle the child. He had best start from the beginning. "Lysbet, this which we call Niew Netherland, was discovered and claimed by the Dutch at the start of this century. It was seen that there could be a rich trade with the natives, but that was not the affair of the States General. So a group of merchants in Amsterdam formed the West India Company and the States General gave them a charter. They could trade; they could buy and sell land; give land if it pleased them. They might also tax as they wished, and in return must defend their settlers. With all this there must be one to represent them, to be the director of this great enterprise. "That is his Excellency, General Petrus Stuyvesant."

"Fort Orange was the first settlement. At the end of the Iroquois trail it was a trading station. Fort Amsterdam, at the mouth of the river, came next. It had a fine harbour for ships and the Company owned ships. There were ships to bring the settlers and the goods they must have, and to carry back the furs. They must also have armed vessels to protect the convoys.

"Dutchmen did not come so quickly as the English did in their provinces. There was trouble in England but none in the Netherlands. Why should men leave their homes and settle in the wilderness? So the Company gave huge grants of land to important people like the Van

Rensselaers of Amsterdam on condition that they would bring simple people to settle the land and cultivate it. People like the Goosens."

Was that all that he must tell her? What of the enmities which had been brought from the old world to the new; the friction between the Dutch and English settlements, each holding their land by right of discovery or possession; both in fear of the French to the north, the Spanish to the south; all encroaching on the native?

This must come to her in time. It was enough now that she should grasp Patria, Niew Netherland, the great Company. She, through force of circumstance, must now be a part of these.

CHAPTER TWO

Niew Amsterdam

❧

THEY APPROACHED NIEW AMSTERDAM LATE THE FOL-
lowing afternoon. Vrouw Kerstedt and her son, who was
in the Burgher Guard, took Lysbet high up on the forward deck where she could see yet be out of the way.
Lysbet felt more at ease there than with the Worshipful Lords and Excellencies.

Vrouw Kerstedt talked to her in the Indian tongue.
How had she learned it, Lysbet asked her. There had
been a great number of Indians about Niew Amsterdam before the massacre, Vrouw Kerstedt told her.

Lysbet was appalled. "Would there be massacre too
in Niew Amsterdam?"

"Not now," Vrouw Kerstedt assured her. "But we do
not make red men as welcome as we did at one time."

Passing an inlet she explained that it was Spuyten
Duyvil Kill which cut Manhattan from the mainland.
At "Manhattan" Lysbet gaped with interest, but it
looked no different from the rest.

At the Mustoota Flats to the east there was a village,
Niew Haarlem, just chartered, Hans told her. He added

that they must have Dutch towns to keep the English out but this Lysbet did not understand.

The land of Manhattan was high but as they came to the end it flattened at the shore with inlets, marshes and beaches. Hans pointed to a stream saying it drained Kalck-Hoek Pond where they fished in summer, skated in winter.

He started to tell of a huge pike that he had caught, but Lysbet's attention had wandered. She had seen the sails of a windmill and beyond it a high steeple.

Hans looked at her rapt face and laughed good-naturedly. "Yes, that is it," he said, proudly. "There is no other such city this side of the water, they say."

There were gardens that ran to the shore. Roofs showed between the trees. Hans pointed to the fort. It had been designed by one of the great Dutch engineers, he told her, though the Company had skimped in the building of it.

The fort's high stone wall, with its four bastions, enclosed the church and windmill. As Lysbet gazed in awe, a flag of white, blue and orange flung out. There was a peal of bells, the roar of cannon. She jumped at the crash of their own guns, returning the salute.

The din kept up while they rounded the tip of Manhattan. Here was the town seen through a jumble of great seagoing vessels and small local craft. It rose from a long, closely built-up street that followed the shore. There were houses of stone and brick, steep pointed roofs, one topped with a high cupola. That was the Stadt Huis. On a point was an especially imposing house surrounded by a garden. The mansion of their Director, built on land confiscated when its owner took to piracy, Hans remarked.

"The point is 'Schreyers Hoek'," he went on, "named after one in Amsterdam. It was where folks gathered to weep when friends sailed for distant parts."

"It's for that this is named the same?" asked Lysbet, with a vision of the tragic scene.

"I expect so," said Hans. "It was a hard voyage at first with much to fear." He pointed to an island, Staten, it was, where Melyn had tried to set up a patroonship like the Van Rensselaers. If he had succeeded the two could have held the North River between them. The Heer Director fought him tooth and nail and the savages too, so the attempt failed.

Lysbet was bewildered with it all yet felt that she was learning fast.

There was added activity, with sailors running back and forth, the captain shouting orders. Then the sails came down, the anchor was dropped and the vessel swung to the tide. Vrouw Kerstedt suggested that they must go to the lower deck, for they soon would be getting off.

The landing craft were swinging over the side and the Heer Director was ready. He had changed his military costume for a fine black suit and broad-brimmed hat with plumes.

As Lysbet climbed down to the deck Domine Megapolensis beckoned to her. "Keep close to my side," he said, "although we may have something of a wait."

But the all-seeing eye of his Excellency was upon them. Speaking to Secretary Van Ruyven that gentleman stepped over. "The Heer Director wishes you to go in the first boat with him. He will make disposition of the child."

Looking a little taken aback, the Domine, with Lysbet, followed him to the boats.

The Heer Director was already halfway down the ladder, his strong arms and staunch spirit overcoming the difficulty of his wooden spike. He was well used to it now, having lost his leg in Forty-six, defending the Company's rights in the West Indies.

To mitigate this blow he had been transferred to this greater post at Niew Amsterdam.

The hostages were standing on the deck, waiting dejectedly. Me too, thought Lysbet, in a sudden panic. This Niew Amsterdam, so overwhelming, what would it do to her? There was no time to question. Domine Megapolensis went over the side and she after him. The same sailor grinned at her.

They sat in the stern of the boat with Burgomaster Van Cortlandt near them to balance the weight. Secretary Van Ruyven and the second Burgomaster were at the bow with his Excellency. Rapidly propelled by oars pulled by four pairs of brawny arms, they approached a long wharf.

A crowd was waiting. This was no ordinary occasion but a triumphant return at the end of a troublesome war. Warned by the noisy welcome all who could either hobble or hop were out. There was old Jacob Van Couwenhoven with his stick; Sarah Bogert and Jan Vinge, the first two born in Niew Netherland, Hendrick Kip, whose son Jacob was aboard the barge, his fat wife, Tryntje and Jacob's French wife, Marie.

Martin Cregier's Tavern commanded a view up the river. His wife was telling how she had already changed her apron and gown before she heard the salvo. Annetje and Blendine Kerstedt, with the baby and ex-baby, were hanging over their fence while their father, Doctor Hans, hurried from his apothecary shop. He was glad his wife was back.

Mevrouw Stuyvesant was waiting at the extremity of their garden with her husband's sisters, Mevrouw Varleth and Mevrouw Backer. Wives of successful merchants, so closely connected with the Director, they could not mingle too commonly with the crowd.

Suusje, Mevrouw Varleth's small step-daughter, ran back and forth between them and the house, reporting the progress of their father's landing to the Stuyvesant boys, Balthazer and Nicholas. Having been disciplined by their tutor, who would not release them, they were hanging out of a rear window.

"He has got a girl with him," Suusje yelled.

"What for?" Balthazer made a face.

"I have got to go back," shouted Suusje. She was a pale, freckled-faced child of eight, her flaxen hair braided in two short pig-tails. Frail from birth she had been petted extravagantly, spoiled and teased by her brother and three step-brothers.

Heer Director Stuyvesant was stumping up the wharf, his party in his wake. On the shore the people were greeting, cheering him. A voice rose above the rest, "God bless your Excellency!"

There had been friction during the first years of his office due to his strict backing of the West India Company's regulations. The liberty-loving Dutchmen had fought him and won the battle. In place of the former antagonism there was respect now. He was loyal, direct, honest, and when danger threatened they could trust him.

He had reached the shore and held up his hand for silence. "My good people," his tones rang out, "I am pleased to inform you that an advantageous peace with the Esopus tribe has been signed. It is our purpose now further to develop this rich part of Niew Netherland, for our growing population has need of what may be raised there and also, in time, if God blesses our efforts, we must be the grainery of our beloved Patria."

"We, representing the Company, will bestow land in this region on favorable terms. There will be established a second settlement under the patronage of Philip Schuyler."

There was a fresh outburst of applause with cheers for Philip Schuyler. Although he lived at Rensselaerswyck, he came often to Niew Amsterdam and was well liked.

This duty finished, Director Stuyvesant strode through the crowd, doffing his hat and bowing. Passing the Custom Huys, his brother-in-law, Mynheer Varleth, stepped out and joined him. This gentleman was not only a rich merchant but Commissioner of Customs.

Suusje, emboldened by the sight of her father, flung open the garden gate and ran out to them.

"Oh, Suusje, not in that crowd," Mevrouw Varleth cried. Following the child she grasped at her shoulder.

His Excellency, escorted by Mynheer Varleth, followed by Domine Megapolensis and Lysbet, quickened his step. Providence had put his sister in his way at just the right moment. They talked, he gesticulating in his positive manner, Mevrouw Varleth evidently protesting. The Domine who, with Lysbet, had been left behind, walked over to join them.

Lysbet stood, her face scarlet, looking to the ground. With a quick instinct she knew they were talking of her, offering her to that grand lady. Why had she left the Goosens to come among fine folks like these, for she was not fit.

The Domine left the group and came back to her. "That gracious lady will try you," he said, "and I could not wish better for you, Lysbet. Mevrouw Varleth will be kind to you and will teach you. In return you must be obedient, honest and truthful. Never give in to your temper."

Hanging her head, Lysbet looked up at him. "They was so hateful, your Honor, plaguing me cruelly from sun-up till sun-down."

Domine Megapolensis had come from the valley of the Rhine where one takes life easily, so patted her shoulder. "We have imps in Niew Amsterdam, Lysbet. If you do not fight them they will not find fun in plaguing you. Remember that."

The Director continued his progress, and the Varleths started for home. Suusje walked demurely, shooting sly glances at Lysbet. Did she wish this girl to live with them? As she could not help it, she wondered how it would affect her. Very little, she thought, for she was bigger than Abram, so could not play with her, but was not grown enough to order her around, like Gertje.

The Varleths lived near the Director. Their house was on the corner of Perel, the street that followed the shore, and Marcktveld, another that led to the fort. It had been built lately, as was shown by the date "1656" laid on its brick face in large copper letters. The roof was peaked and the stoop high, with the door rich in ornament.

Opening a gate at the side they walked to the back. As there was a house next them it was a narrow path, with flowers planted on the fence side. There was a garden beyond but Lysbet did not have a chance to look at it. Mevrouw Varleth opened a door, then turned, took hold of her arm and pushed her in.

It was an entry with hooks for cloaks and caps. Beyond was a great kitchen, which they entered. A low fire burned, and smoked, implements hung on the cranes, and stood on the hearth, but there was no sign of cooking. In the center of the room was a long trencher table, a dozen or more stools drawn up to it. There were gaily painted settles and dressers, these overflowing with pewter and china. Beautiful brass and copper pots and pans hung on the walls.

A flight of winding stairs were in one of its corners, a door to a second kitchen was opposite. There was no one about, but a half-sliced loaf stood on the table, and a large pat of butter.

"No sign of Gertje," said Mevrouw Varleth. "In fact I should say they were all at the landing."

Her husband laughed. "Gertje is young. Wan and Yoff? Well, they are young in heart."

"I must see to this child," Mevrouw Varleth went on. "One of Gertje's outgrown frocks may fit her as to length, though the width will be absurd."

Mynheer Varleth, with Suusje, looked at Lysbet. "Gertje would make two of her," he said, then shooed a bumblebee from the butter. "Gertje should have covered it over."

"There is much that she should do but does not," said his wife, then went to a winding flight of stairs in one of the corners and tramped up them with a decided tread.

Mynheer Varleth glanced again at the new member of his family. She stood stiff, uncertain just what to do.

"Sit down till Mevrouw calls you," he said kindly. Then telling Suusje to make herself agreeable he took a pipe from a shelf and went to the garden.

Suusje did not want to be left alone with this strange girl and she did not feel like making herself agreeable. Instead she went to the table and pounded the bread-knife on the board.

She may cut herself, thought Lysbet, but will not take it kindly if I tell her.

A door opened at the back and a face peered cautiously in. Round blue eyes roved about, then fastened on Lysbet in surprise. The door opened wider and the whole girl appeared. She was short, plump, with cheeks as round as her eyes and fair hair braided neatly and wound about her head.

"La!" she shrilled, darting at Suusje. "Give me that knife!" Wiping it on her apron, she vigorously resumed her slicing.

"I'll tell your step-mother," she said, darkly.

"I will tell her that you wiped the knife on your apron," retorted Suusje.

At that critical moment a call sounded from above.
"Lysbet."

"My step-mother wants you," said Suusje importantly.
"You go up that same way."

As Lysbet mounted the stairs she felt the girl's eyes
upon her. That is Gertje, she thought. When she re-

turned some time later in a bodice and skirt noticeably tucked in, she saw from Gertje's expression that she had heard all that Suusje knew.

Going to one of the dressers Mevrouw took out plates and Gertje spread them.

"Will ye let me help too?" Lysbet ventured timidly.

Gertje thrust forward a handful of knives and spoons but Mevrouw Varleth interposed. "No, Gertje, not yet." Turning to Suusje, she told her to take Lysbet to the garden, to show her the flowers which had come from Patria.

To Lysbet, used to unlimited space, it seemed a small garden but beautiful beyond anything that she had ever seen. The blue waters of the harbour were beyond, and in the beds, a riot of color, flowers that she had never dreamed of, trees new to her.

"Peach," said Suusje, picking a tiny green nubbin, "but it is not ripe yet. The trees have not been planted long so have not had time to grow." She pointed to others. "The wild trees were here." She told then about George and Thomas Baxter, whose land this had been. George had tried to raise an English flag in a Dutch town and his brother was a pirate. "He was not always a pirate," she said, "and when we were at war with the English it was well. But after that was over he did not want to stop."

Mynheer Varleth came from a summerhouse and pointed out special flowers. Most of them had come from Amsterdam but there was one clump of white flowers with yellow centers, English daisies which he had brought from Hartford in the Connecticut valley.

"He lived there before those hateful English crowded in," said Suusje. "My grandfather and Aunt Judith live there now."

Her father gave her a warning pinch. The child was English.

A war-whoop sounded from the house but with no ill intent here. It was only Mevrouw Varleth's sons, the Bayard boys, calling them to supper. There were three of them just released from their Latin School. Abram, Suusje's own brother, still went to the primary school and came in later.

Mynheer Varleth took his place at the head of the lavishly spread board. Gertje motioned to Lysbet and pulled out a stool for her at the low end. There was a scraping of stools as they all stood up for the blessing. A black man and woman came in from the rear kitchen and bent their heads then went back to their own supper.

These young city gentlemen seemed just as hungry as Dirck and Jan Goosen had been. Great mouthfuls went down the ravenous throats. Wild turkey, sausage, clotted cream and sweetmeats, mountains of bread, melted like butter in August.

Under Gertje's patronising care Lisbet herself ate as she had not done for weeks, for with food scarce and whoops of hatred sounding outside how could one eat.

She took shy glances at the family. Suusje sat next to her father and Abram next to her. He was older than she but like her. Then came two almost grown; these were Balthazer and Petrus Bayard. Nick Bayard, with dark hair and eyes like his mother's, sat next her on the other side. A good looking youth of sixteen, he was the gayest of the three.

With bread heaped high in one hand, a scallion in the other, he took big bites, and went into fits of laughter telling how he and Stephanus Van Cortlandt had climbed out of a window when Curtius' back was turned and gone to see the landing.

Suusje piped up gleefully. "When you got back what did he do to you?"

Munching his scallion, Nick shrugged his shoulders. "Naught that we minded."

His mother broke in, "This fine professor who charges a whole beaver skin a year but cannot keep order!"

"He complains that his hands are tied by you mothers, objecting to his floggings," Mynheer Varleth laughed.

"He laid on too heavy," Mevrouw Varleth protested. "Poor Nick could not sit for near a week with the welts, and the bear grease we had to use."

There was a whoop from his brothers and a laugh in which Gertje joined boisterously. Nick jumped up and walked around his stool, then sat again.

"Our uncle, as usual, carried himself like a Muscovy Czar."

"Nick, that is too much," said his mother. "Gather up your plate and finish your supper in the garden."

There was a long twilight, another supper by candle-light, then a general mounting the stairs to bed. Lysbet went up a second flight this time for she would share a room with Gertje. Their bed was built into the wall with doors that they could shut on winter nights. Gertje said that her bed was the lower one and that Lysbet must climb.

Mevrouw had laid out a night shift of Suusje's which, although short, fitted Lysbet more comfortably. With a good night to Gertje she pulled herself up and sank in, drawing the quilt over her.

"I am coming too, so move up," said Gertje, climbing in after her and settling herself with a grunt. "Lysbet," she whispered, "I'm glad you've come, for now I'll have one to bear me company. The Varleths is proud. 'Cause they's kin of the Director they think they's somebody." She rambled on. She and her brother Hans had been sent from Amsterdam in a shipload of orphans three years ago. Hans was getting rich, trading in furs but this was as far as she had got.

Mevrouw Varleth looked fine enough but wait till Lysbet did aught to anger her. The food was plenty but if one got hungry between meals ye must help yourself unbeknownst.

You should not talk so of people who were kind to you. Lysbet had been taught this early by her squaw-mother. Besides, she did not want Gertje in her bed squeezing her to the wall. "I am so sleepy I do not want to talk," she finally said.

"If that is how you feel," snapped Gertje. She heaved over the side pulling the quilt with her. Lysbet heard her muttering from below.

Letting her own head sink to the pillow she heard the watchman's cry as if in a dream. "Nine o'clock. Fair weather."

CHAPTER THREE

Lysbet Settles In

❧

LYSBET DID NOT WEAR GERTJE'S OUTGROWN GARMENTS
long. Mevrouw Varleth produced material from one of
her chests and Metje Greveraat, a little old woman on
Beaver Street, made new clothes. The Director, as his
contribution, paid her for the work.

When they were finished Lysbet was dressed and sent
to his Excellency to show herself and thank him for his
kindness. He pinched her cheek and said he would not
have known her. He then said that she must get some
fat on her bones and sent word to his sister to feed her up.

The lack of fat on her bones did not bother Lysbet.
This bewildering new experience was crowding in upon
her; there was so much to understand all at once.

Domine Megapolensis and the Director had both said
that she must go to school and learn to read and write,
but Mevrouw Varleth thought it better to wait until she
learned her letters at least. The other pupils might laugh
at this tall child's ignorance.

Ægidius Luyck, a learned young man who had lately
come from Leyden to be the Stuyvesants' tutor, offered

to start her. There was a wistful look in her eyes that roused his interest and even with his rather troublesome charges, the time hung heavy on his hands.

Lysbet heard the astonishing fact that the world was round, with tales of daring exploration to prove it. She was shown maps with great bodies of land that she had never dreamed of, heard stories of their people, stories of the seas and the monsters that swam them, stories of the stars, the sun, the moon.

She learned numbers and letters and how to write them and how to use them, which opened up another world. Ægidius said that her mind soaked in learning like thirsty ground.

The Delft tiles set in about the fireplace had pictures from the Bible with the name and numbers showing their places. Lysbet stole into the sacred fore-room one day to look for them in the great silver bound book. Mevrouw Varleth was visiting a neighbor but her portrait, painted with her first husband, stared at Lysbet from the wall and made her feel guilty. But she could not resist. Turning to Genesis she found the story of Adam and Eve and tried to pick out the words.

Gertje had followed her. "I'll tell 'em," she bawled gleefully, "I'll tell 'em what ye are doin'."

"Tell if it please you," said Lysbet, shutting the book carefully. She never touched it again but listened eagerly when Mynheer Varleth read it or Domine Megapolensis in church.

He, responsible for her religious education, had given her a catechism and taught her Article 1 of the Belgic Confession of Faith. "God the everlasting fountain of all good." He had said that this would be enough for the present but for her to think of it.

Lysbet did think of it and she wondered if God was

not also the "Great Spirit" of the Indians but did not dare to ask.

The church was named for Saint Nicholas. It was long with a high ceiling and its bells were Spanish, captured in a raid on Puerto Rico. There were eight steps to the pulpit where the Domine stood and preached and Mynheer Curtius, the master of the Latin School, sat at the foot of them, leading the Psalms and turning the hour glass. The front pews were reserved for the Lord Director and city officials with their families. They entered with ceremony, all the congregation standing, and were accompanied by slaves or white servants carrying the cushions for them to sit on.

Gertje, in her grudging way, scoffed at all this. She told Lysbet that she should see Oude Kerk in Amsterdam with its thirty chapels, its windows with pictures of saints and angels, its big marble tombs.

"As I'm no' likely to see that I'll content myself wi' this," said Lysbet drily.

It was especially hard for Balthazer and Nicholas Stuyvesant to sit so high and under the eye of the Latin master for they were restless boys. They had been over-indulged by their gentle mother in an effort to soften their father's stern discipline.

The Director had been too busy with his duties at Curaçao to marry early but, after the loss of his leg, had been forced to go home for treatment, and while visiting his widowed sister, Madame Bayard, at Alphen, near the medical center of Leyden, he had succumbed to the youthful charms of Judith Bayard, her sister-in-law. The Bayards were of the line of Chevalier Bayard, that knight *"sans peur et sans reproche"* but had been driven from France by religious differences.

When his Excellency sailed with his bride to take his post at Niew Netherland, Madame Bayard and her three sons accompanied them. She wished her brother's help in bringing up her fatherless boys but had since substituted Mynheer Varleth, a man of high character, a distinguished citizen of their expanding city.

It was a big family connection: the Backers, who had come later, the Varleths, the Stuyvesants, the Bayards, bound to the Stuyvesants by a double tie. With their Balthazers and their Nicholas's Lysbet could not keep them straight. There was visiting back and forth and even the Director sat on their stoops or walked in their gardens. He knew every herb and flower for nothing was too small for his interest.

There were others who came to sit on the Varleths' stoop or in their summerhouse. The Kerstedts from across Marcktveld, Burgomaster Van Cortlandt and his wife Anneken from Brower Street, the Van Der Veens, who lived next door and other neighbors.

Lysbet noted how they talked, and tried to improve her own speech. When they used words she did not understand she asked Suusje, Abram or Ægidius what they meant. She was not shy with them as she was with the Bayard boys.

The summer was hot and dry. Yoff brought water from the well near the fort to keep the garden green. The flowers, coming up in quick succession, were babies to the big, soft-spoken man. He weeded and dug and Lysbet gradually got into the way of helping him. She was used to outdoor life and being in the house too much irked her. She loved to see the great vessels sailing in and out, their white canvas billowing and the myriads of birds of which the harbour was full. She loved the salt air and the fresh smell. If there was but a whiff of breeze Schreyers Hoek would get it.

One day Yoff told her in his halting tongue how he had been brought from far off Africa to Curaçao and later up here. He described the horrors of that trip, the parting from his people. But he would not go back, he said. The Varleths had given him his freedom and they were good to him.

Lysbet would often go with him to the Stuyvesant's North River bouwerie and carry back baskets of fruit or vegetables while he carried the milk. They passed the fort and open plain,* where the soldiers drilled and the cattle market was held, the burying ground and then went up the Heere Weg,† a street not yet paved. The bouwerie had once belonged to the Company but the

* The Battery.
† Broadway.

Director had bought it. There were gardens and orchards with barns for the Stuyvesants', Varleths' and Backers' beasts, and stys for the pigs as he wished to stop the practice of having these creatures run the streets, picking rubbish from the gutters. Other enclosures penned in various little wild animals that the boys kept as pets.

The city wall that ran from river to river bound in the bouwerie to the north.

Yoff told Lysbet that it was to keep the English out. This Lysbet could not understand. There were many of the English living inside the wall and in the towns across the East River.

It was a half holiday and the Bayard and Stuyvesant boys were there, paddling about in their canoe. Seeing Petrus away from them for a moment, she plucked up her courage to ask him. "Why did they build a wall to keep the English out when there were so many within?"

"The ones who live within are our own people," he told her. "Many of them enjoy our easier way of life. The ones we wished to keep out are our greedy neighbors of Massachusetts, Plymouth, Connecticut. They know we have the pick of the whole coast, a harbour that our Captains tell us is unexcelled, rich fertile land, a navigable river.

"When England and the Netherlands were at war in fifty-five they planned to make that an excuse to take us over. We heard rumors and hurriedly built that wall but, luckily, the war ended just then."

Balthazer Stuyvesant had joined them and now broke in angrily. "But they had already taken all our land to the east, torn down the sign of the States General and carved a fool's head in its place."

"It was a fool that did it," said Petrus, then seeing Lysbet's eye upon him, explained. "It was a sign claiming the Connecticut River and the land to the west of it. The Dutch had built a fort where Hartford is now, but the Company had never sent settlers to hold it. Settlers from Massachusetts had seeped in and while they would have been welcome to come as Dutch subjects these wished not that. They wanted to throw off the rule of even Massachusetts and form their own colonies of Connecticut, New Haven, and another group to the east, Providence Plantations."

"When our uncle came as director, he must make the best of it. Squabbling over wild land here might bring war at home. So he made a treaty with these squatters. If they would go no further there and on the Long Island, the Dutch would give up the land."

"But they say now that this treaty means nothing," said Balthazer, sarcastically.

"Because it has never been ratified in Europe," said Petrus. "What with the Company's neglect and the beheading of the English King upsetting things generally."

"The beheading of the English King!" Lysbet could hardly believe her ears.

Petrus laughed at her face. "Some say he well deserved it."

Balthazer objected to that. "My father does not hold with upstarts beheading lawful rulers no matter what they have done."

"Well, now that his son is back we hope that both the High Mightinesses will get at that Hartford treaty," said Petrus. "Then we can thumb our noses at Connecticut."

Lysbet hoped that her people had not been these squatters. No one seemed to recall that it was, after all, Indian land and it had been theirs always.

There were two bastions in the wall, one called "Hollandia" the other "Zeelandia," a Water Poort at the end of Lang de Waal, a way that followed the river picking up Hoogh. The Landt Poort * was at the Heere Weg, a stone's throw from the bouwerie. These two were shut at night but open in the day.

Beyond the Landt Poort was the great bouwerie of Damen of the "Bloody Hands." He was dead now but had done mischief in his day, having been chiefly to blame in the massacre of hundreds of helpless River Indians, taking refuge with the whites from their enemies the Mohawks. North of Damen's was "Lord's Waste" a common pasture for the animals.

* City gate.

Picking up the Heere Weg an old Indian trail led through it all, twisting to avoid Kalck-Hoek Pond,* continuing up the island taking in a large property which the Director owned and used for heavy planting, then five or six miles up, Niew Haarlem. There was not much passing this way except on Market Day and even then, much was brought by boat. This was also the case with the produce from the Long Island, for there was a ferry beyond the wall with a scow roomy enough for beasts.

Lysbet would sometimes beg Yoff to return by the Schaape Weytie † inside the wall. It was a hill ending in the swamp that was drained by the canal Heere Gracht. Even in the drought there were flowers, marsh elder, marsh marigold, and Lysbet picked them adding them to her load.

From the Heere Gracht, where the Beckers lived, they would generally turn to Brower Street, for Mevrouw Varleth did not like the girls to go on Perel Street much when the boats were in.

There were great Dutch men-of-war and carrying ships that came to Niew Amsterdam, English, French and Dutch privateers, smaller ships plying between Virginia, Mary-land and New England, preferring the sheltered waters of the sound to open sea, and making excuse to stop at Niew Amsterdam.

* City Hall Park.
† Sheep Pasture.

The sailors swarmed the water front and the taverns, throwing about florins, guilders, pieces of eight midst a jumble of tongues, French, English, even the hated Spanish and Portuguese. Niew Amsterdamers winked at their roughness and welcomed their silver, doing most of their own trading in wampum and beaver skins as the Company kept them close.

A ship sailed for Curaçao and the Indian hostages were brought from the dungeon at the fort and put aboard. They were marched down Marcktveld * surrounded by a hooting mob. Suusje, Lysbet and Gertje heard the excitement and rushed to the gate.

Suusje and Gertje mocked with the rest but Lysbet, knowing how these proud men might feel pitied in spite of herself.

Marritje and Jannetje Lockerman were hanging over the gate of the Van Der Veens, next door. They were the step-sisters of Mevrouw Van Der Veen, and daughters of Govert Lockerman, the richest man in town. He had come to Niew Amsterdam as a cook's mate, then made a fortune in trading. Lysbet had heard Nick tell the story of his yacht *The Hope* which was the first packet ship up the river.

"It was in the old days," he had begun, "when Rensselaerswyck acknowledged no authority but its own. They had fortified Beeren Island near our Fort Orange and said no other trader should pass.

* Whitehall.

"*The Hope* slipped through but on its return trip they were waiting. 'Lower thy colors!' they shouted. 'For who should I do so?' Lockerman shouted back. 'For the staple right of Rensselaerswyck,' they shouted again.

"Nick had leaped to his feet then. 'I lower not my colors for any save the Prince of Orange and their High Mightinesses, the States General.' A shot broke a rope and the colors came down. Lockerman caught them and thrust them high. 'Fire again, ye dogs!' he yelled. A second shot rang out but did not hit them. Exulting, they continued down the river."

Lysbet thought of this story now as she looked admiringly at the girls. They were pretty. It was hard to see which one was the prettiest. They had fine clothes and wore amber beads at their throats. Their house, situated at the place where Hoogh ran into Waal, was larger than any other and their garden the best in town. There were other tales of their father. He had once gotten into trouble trading guns to Indians, and was not blameless at the time of Damen's villainy.

As time went on Lysbet heard more of the English King who had been beheaded, and of his son, a second Charles, who had just been called back to his father's throne. As an exile he had lived at the Hague. All, from the Director down, hoped for better Dutch and English relations.

CHAPTER FOUR

Suusje

❦

HIS EXCELLENCY, DIRECTOR GENERAL STUYVESANT, SAT
in the summerhouse at the foot of his garden overlook-
ing the harbour. With him was Secretary Van Ruyven.

Smoking and enjoying the peaceful autumn sunshine,
they discussed an order recently come from the Company recalling the soldiers sent over at the time of the
Esopus war.

If carried out this order would reduce the entire garrison of the Province to a mere handful of men and place
the Director in a difficult position. It is hard to bargain
with aggressive neighbors when there is no force behind
one's word. The situation required more than tact.

The Director grew angry as he talked. The Company
had sent out its colonists with a promise of military protection. Now they said defend yourselves! If need arise
enlist the redskins as allies! "Madness," his Excellency
said. "Once let these vainglorious warriors suspect we
need their help and the vaunted 'Chain of Friendship'
snaps like a blade of grass."

He broke off and turned his attention to his son,

Nicholas, who was scrambling up the rocks below the summerhouse.

"Have a care for those new breeches, boy," he shouted. "They do not grow upon trees, and get up to the house quickly. Your mother has an errand."

Nicholas came to the door of the summerhouse. "I did not know anyone was here, sir," he said. "May I get my fishing tackle? It is there in the corner."

"You will have no time for fishing this afternoon. Now, trot!"

Nicholas lagged towards the house. His brother and the other boys were waiting on the wharf for him and the fishing tackle. He had managed badly and there was no help for him now. He knew what the errand was. A wagon load of crab apples and late garden truck had come over from the bouwerie and his mother was sending some to the Varleths and Beckers.

"First you must borrow the Varleths' old baby-wagon," his mother said. "It carries more than a hand-barrow. Maybe you can get Abram to help, or one of the girls. I can not spare anyone from the kitchen just now."

At the Varleths' Lysbet and Abram were pressed into service. They were dispatched across with Suusje's long out-grown baby-wagon, used now for purposes such as this. They returned alone dragging the loaded wagon between them. Nicholas had escaped.

"He said Balthazer and the other boys were waiting," Lysbet explained to Mevrouw Varleth. "Mevrouw

Stuyvesant said you was to take what you want. The rest be for Mevrouw Backer."

"It is far too heavy a load for you children to haul up Brower Street hill," the Mevrouw decided. "Gertje had best take your place, Lysbet, and you can help Wan with these apples."

Gertje, who was helping unload, jumped for joy. Anything to get away from the kitchen drudgery. She almost snatched the wagon-tongue from Lysbet's hand.

"I want to go," Suusje had followed Gertje out. "I want to ride in my cart again."

"Her weight won't make no odds," said Gertje, lifting Suusje to the top of the load. There she sat on a giant pumpkin, her feet in the apple basket. "We won't go up Brower Hill. We'ull go along Perel and up by th'Canal."

The wagon started with a jerk, and Suusje swayed perilously. "Hi yi," she shouted. "Go fast!"

"Hold tight, Suusje," called Mevrouw Varleth as she turned back to the house. "Come, Lysbet, and latch the gate after them. I do not want Couwenhovens' porkers rooting up the garden again."

Lysbet lingered, watching the top-heavy wagon bounce over the cobbles till it got out of her sight. She would have liked the little go as much as Gertje.

Mevrouw Varleth appeared at the door again. "Lysbet, you must run after them. Suusje went off with neither hood nor shawl. She catches cold so easily. Take this cloak and see that she puts it on. The breeze off the water is fresh."

"Oh, yes, Mevrouw, I'll run," cried Lysbet, her face lighting up. She dashed off.

Mevrouw Varleth watched her, half smiling. "There is the gate unlatched again. Well."

I will catch them before they cross the wagon-bridge, Lysbet thought, but how these long skirts hold me back.

The boys, balked of their fishing, were idling about the town-wharf. Nick Bayard sang out as she ran by. "Hey, Giblets, what's yer hurry?" He still made game of her Wiltwyck Dutch.

She reached the Heere Graft where the little foot-bridge spanned the mouth of the canal. It was a flimsy affair, taken down every autumn to escape the winter gales and set up again each spring. The tide was falling and was rushing out with considerable force. The wooden piles which formed the sides of the canal were exposed, slimy with green seaweed.

Fifty yards up the Heere Graft was the wagon-bridge, with a ramp and hand-rail. Gertje and Abram, still running, had reached the turn. Jerked sidewise, the full weight of the haul bore down on Abram. He stumbled. Gertje plunged ahead. The wagon swerved and Suusje with a squeal of terror, was tossed clear of the rail and into the rushing tide. The pumpkin bounded after. Apples flew far and wide.

Lysbet stopped. At first she did not grasp what had

happened. Then Suusje's scream and a flash of the child's red dress in the swirling water, told the tale. Back she raced for the foot-bridge, tugging at the drawstring of her skirt as she ran.

The tide was sweeping very fast. She must reach the bridge before Suusje was carried beyond it and into the tide-rips of the inlet.

Gertje was screaming now. People were running. Abram was tearing down the Heere Graft. Lysbet stood in the middle of the bridge, twenty feet above the water. She dropped her skirt and stepped clear of it. No time to unbuckle her heavy shoes. There! There was a flash of red to the right! She jumped. As she went under something touched her. She clutched wildly and missed.

She came up gasping from the chill water. Suusje was near her, not three feet away. A couple of strong strokes and Lysbet had her by the arm, had dragged her head above the water.

"I've got ye, Suusje. Don't choke me!" Suusje coughed and sputtered and stopped struggling. Light as the child was, Lysbet could do little more than hold her own against the current.

The boys on the wharf had heard the screaming, had seen Lysbet jump. Canoes, skiffs, a plenty of small boats, hauled above the tide mark, were at hand. Nick Bayard had a canoe in the water immediately fighting against the tide. Stephanus Van Cortlandt and the Cregier boy followed in a row boat.

Other boys with better intentions than sense began throwing boat-hooks, oars and paddles at the two bobbing heads. Luckily they all fell short.

Balthazer Stuyvesant stood poised, taking careful aim with a heavy oar. One of the older boys grasped his arm. "Do you want to brain the girl? Here, let me have it."

Quickly he knotted a length of rope to the oar and hurled it harpoonlike into the water in front of the girls. With a quick thrust of her free arm, Lysbet got a hold on the oar, a grip on the rope.

"That's it," came a shout as the line tightened. Many hands were laid on and a few moments later the girls were dragged to safety and the center of an excited, chattering crowd. It was the time of day when work was over and folk were at leisure to stand about and enjoy any little happening.

Lysbet, dripping and dirty, soggy hair dangling, her short blue linen petticoat clinging about her legs, was covered with shame. With her Indian training this exploit had been trifling, and here she was, looking a sight before them all.

"Here is your skirt, Giblets." It was the young fellow who had thrown the oar. Lysbet knew who he was, Cornelis Jansen, an apprentice of Heer Duyckink, the glassmaker. He was tall and straight with warm brown hair. His voice was serious but his dark eyes twinkled as he held out her skirt.

"Thank ye," Lysbet said with what dignity she could,

and added, lifting her chin a little, "My name's Lysbet."

"Your pardon," he said gravely, "Lysbet what?"

She could have bitten her tongue out. How could she acknowledge that she did not know her own name! The teasing laughter died out of young Jansen's eyes. He knew her story. Everyone did, but more than most he could sympathise. When only a year old he had lost his parents in an Indian raid, revenge for Damen's treachery.

Before he could say anything Abram spoke up. He had been in time to see the rescue, and wanted to assert his claim to Lysbet as well as Suusje. "Her name is Lysbet Varleth," he said loudly.

"No, t'is not," Lysbet began but a firm hand was laid on her shoulder.

"Come, Lysbet, you are shivering." Mynheer Varleth had been enjoying a quiet pipe with Mynheer Backer on the high steps of the Custom House facing the wharf. He had watched the show with mild amusement not knowing the prominent part his family were playing until Suusje was pulled in like a drowned kitten.

With Suusje on his shoulder, Lysbet by the hand and Abram prancing in front, Mynheer Varleth turned homewards followed by a murmur of congratulation and approval.

Meanwhile Gertje had stopped screaming and watched the progress of the event with a good deal of anxiety. When she saw that all was well she proceeded to straighten the wagon and gather the scattered load. The pumpkin was gone beyond recall but the apples and a couple of squash were none the worse for the spill. I'll be blamed, for all this, she thought sullenly as she started on.

Mevrouw Backer was standing at her door, shading her eyes against the setting sun. "What was all that screaming about?" she asked as Gertje drew up.

"No great hap," the girl told her. "Suusje fell in the canal and got pulled out again."

"No great hap, do you say?" exclaimed the Mevrouw indignantly. She had four youngsters of her own running about.

Gertje spent some time in the Backer kitchen, enjoying a glass of buttermilk and a mouthful of gossip with the Backers' slave girl, Zoe. It was dusk by the time she reached home. She put the cart away in the tool-shed and slipped quietly into the kitchen where the evening meal was preparing. She took a knife and began cleaning some fish that lay on the table. If she had hoped to escape notice, she failed, but Wan was too eager to tell the news for more than a sharp, "Where yu'be dis long time?" before bursting out with the story.

It seemed Suusje fell in the canal and Lysbet had swum out and saved her or so Mynheer Collector said. He had brought them both home, dripping wet, and Mevrouw, when she heard what had been, had kissed Lysbet and called her brave girl, and Sussje had sneezed

and been put to bed, and Lysbet had come to the kitchen
for hot milk and had told them how it was.

"It was only that I jump in quick and hold Suusje till
somebody pull us out like two big fishes," Lysbet had
said.

"Lysbet talk small," Yoff spoke up from the chimney-
seat, "but not many folksies jump in water that away.
She got guts."

"She's got luck," muttered Gertje as she jabbed savagely at the slippery fish in her hand.

Suusje had caught a heavy cold and for some days, while the fever lasted, Doctor Kerstedt came, and Mevrouw Varleth kept her in bed. The child was sensible enough to understand the danger she had been in and that Lysbet's strong arms had saved her, and now it was Lysbet she wanted every minute of the day. Lysbet must sit with her, bring up her meals, play with her, tell her stories. No one else would do.

When she was well again it was the same. She followed Lysbet about. "Play with me, Lysbet." "Tell me a story, Lysbet. Tell me about the bear in the cave. Tell about the baby beavers." No one could tell such wonderful tales as Lysbet. Even Abram listened, spellbound. Neither his cousins, the Stuyvesant boys, nor his step-brothers, the Bayards, had had such exciting adventures.

Happy to please them, Lysbet racked her brains for stories but she never told of that cry, "Run, Elizabeth," or of Little Beaver.

It was not long after this that she was sent to regular school. Ægidius Luyck assured Mevrouw Varleth that she could hold her own with any girl of her age in Niew Amsterdam. He might almost have said any boy in Niew Amsterdam.

Mevrouw Varleth smiled. "That would be saying a great deal, Ægidius, considering the little savage she was six months ago."

So one bright morning Lysbet set out with Abram

for Evert Pieterson's school on Brower Street. She had not heard Heer Luyck's high praise of her scholarship but she had a blue cloth jacket and brown petticoat and new leather shoes which gave a lift to her courage.

The shoes were a present from Mynheer Varleth, and the dress from his Excellency, the Director, who continued to be interested in his protégée.

He told Mevrouw Varleth that some day he would have a serious search made for her kinsfolk, if any might be left alive, though truth to tell it was hard to know where to look in all the vast wildernesses around them. He would bespeak the help of the Connecticut Council at the earliest opportunity.

School was less imposing than Lysbet expected. It was kept in one long, narrow room, with benches at either end and the schoolmaster's desk on a little platform in the middle. Heer Pieterson enrolled Lysbet in his book, asked a few questions and placed her on a bench with three other girls near her own age.

Lysbet knew them all by sight, Janneken Loper, granddaughter of the Melyn that the Director had fought, Maryje Van Couwenhoven, and Annetje Kerstedt, Hans' sister.

With a rush of surprise and relief Lysbet knew that she was on the pay-side of the room, that Mynheer Varleth had paid the beaver skin for her just as he had for Abram. Radiant with happiness, she looked around her, and Annetje Kerstedt smiled back and offered the loan of her tablets.

Suusje had not gone to school yet. Her step-mother thought it was high time but her father put it off from term to term, hating to lose his baby, he said.

A few mornings after Lysbet started Suusje decided. "I am going to school," she announced, kicking off her slippers and delving into a heap of shoes behind the door.

"You will not like it," Abram told her. "You are such a dunce, you will have to sit on the A B C bench with Jacob Lockerman."

"I will not. I am going to sit with Katryntje Van Cortlandt."

"You do not even know your letters."

"Do too. I can say them faster than you can." This she proceeded to prove with her eyes tight shut, shouting at the top of her lungs. Abram, a few letters behind, was in hot pursuit.

"What goes on there?" called Mynheer Varleth, from the breakfast table.

Lysbet stuck her head through the entry door. "It is Suusje, Mynheer. She wants to go to school. She is saying her letters."

"If she says her letters like that in school, she will get her knuckles rapped," said Nick, laughing.

"It is because Lysbet is going," said Mevrouw Varleth, selecting a rosy cheeked apple for Suusje to take. She stood smiling as the three students ran off and turned the corner to the alley.

CHAPTER FIVE

Saint Nicholas' Eve

❦

IT WAS DAYBREAK ON A DECEMBER MORNING AND A LIGHT
snow was falling over the house-tops and the harbour
of Niew Amsterdam. The two vessels that were to carry
the soldiers back to the Netherlands lay in the East River
waiting the tide. The men had embarked the evening
before, the farewells were said. Only a few idlers had
gathered on the Hoek to watch them.

The Director did the wailing now, stumping up and
down his garden walk. The Company had ignored his
protests and the men must go.

The first of the outward bound vessels, all her canvas
spread, gathered speed as she cleared the Hoek and came
abreast the Fort. The cannon barked a salute, and the
colors were dipped in return. The ship squared off on
the first leg of her long journey. The second transport
followed.

His Excellency shrugged and turned abruptly, went
out by a side-gate and across to the Varleths. It was early
for a call but he stood on no ceremony with his sister's
household.

Lysbet and Gertje were laying the table when the noise of the cannon jarred the house. They watched the two vessels gliding like ghosts in the snow-storm and were still at the window as the Director came up the path.

Gertje grunted and flopped on the hearth to coax the fire. The soles of her naked feet stuck out from under her short petticoat. Lysbet opened the door, thankful that she was properly dressed.

The Director paid no heed to her or to Gertje but strode into the room, shaking the loose snow from his clothes.

"What, nobody down yet? Ho there, Varleth, you have company to breakfast!"

Mynheer Varleth was already there and before his greetings were over the Mevrouw appeared. Lysbet saw the swift glance she cast around. The slovenly Gertje had retreated to the back-kitchen and otherwise there was nothing to blush for.

They sat to breakfast at last and over the meat pasties and fried fish, the Director explained the object of his visit. To offset the loss of the regular soldiers, he meant to enlarge the Burgher Guard, to form a new company. He planned a mounted troop to defend the Dutch half of the Long Island. He could get fine Spanish horses from Curaçao. He counted on his nephews to assist in these schemes, on the two oldest at any rate. Nick was too young.

"I should say so!" exclaimed Nick's mother. In her opinion they were all three nothing but school boys. They should stick to their books.

His Excellency admitted that education was of the utmost importance. On the other hand, the common weal was in some cases —— and so on, at great length.

Mynheer Varleth agreed and pointed out that some few hours each week for military training should not be too distracting. In the end Balthazer and Petrus Bayard headed the list of recruits for the new company. In token of his satisfaction their Uncle would give each of them a rifle, new style ones with long barrels. Poor Nick's cup of woe was full.

A day or two later came Saint Nicholas' Eve, on Wednesday, a half holiday. Lysbet spent it in the kitchen, where Mevrouw Varleth was overseeing the mixing and baking of great batches of cakes. Lysbet seeded raisins and pounded almonds till her arms ached.

Suusje helped too, in lesser ways, nibbling sugar, licking spoons, chattering happily. This was Saint Nicholas' Eve—Tonight the good Bishop would come—down the chimney—with his bag of toys.

Balthazer and Petrus had gone duck shooting on the Hackingh * meadows to try their new weapons. At the last moment Nick, cheered by the loan of his step-father's gun, had gone with them. They got home late, the old flat-bottomed skiff triumphantly laden. The Varleths

* Hackensack.

would live on wild goose and duck for weeks to come.

Nick was soaking wet. "He thought he was a retrie-ver," Balthazer said. "Every time a bird dropped, he jumped in."

Nick laughed. "Only once, and I fell in. I did not jump."

The Van Der Veens were giving a "cake-pasting" party that evening and the whole Varleth family were in-vited. Even Yoff and Wan were to go, to help serve and enjoy a share of the feast.

It was growing late and time they all spruced up, put on their Sunday clothes. But the boys lingered in the kitchen, talking over their day, boasting a little. There came a knocking at the back door. Lysbet opened it and in came two rough-looking fellows, in leather shirts and breeches, Gertje's brother, Hans, and his partner, Joris Klenck. This was Lysbet's first acquaintance with them and she was not impressed. Hans was like Gertje, blue-eyed and fair, only where her chin was obstinate, his was weak. The other, Joris, was older. He had a mean, foxy face. They both looked dirty and reeked of badly cured skins. In spite of all this, Gertje seemed glad to see them.

They had come down the river that morning with a canoe-load of pelts to trade for winter supplies. Hans had wanted to know how his sister fared.

When Mevrouw Varleth learned of their arrival, she came out to the back-kitchen to speak to them. She told

Gertje that she need not go to the Van Der Veens that evening but could stay at home and get up a supper for her guests. She could take a couple of ducks, or pigeons for a pie, as she chose. They should have sausage and beer and spice-cake besides.

"Gertje has plenty of faults," the Mevrouw remarked to her husband later, "but she is devoted to Hans and I like her for it."

"Sisterly devotion is something," said Mynheer Varleth, "though I saw little of it in her expression when you said she must stay at home and cook tonight. Between ourselves," he added, "those young men have not too good a reputation in my department. Bos-lopers, illegal traders, we suspect, but we can not pin it on them."

Lysbet left this unsavory company to tidy herself and comb out her hair. She regretted that it was not long enough to braid. The blue jacket looked almost new.

As she ran downstairs, Mevrouw Varleth called her. She had a small collar of cambric and lace in her hand.

"Your jacket needs something to dress it up," she said. "This was mine when I was your age and I want you to have it now."

Lysbet looked up, her face radiant. "Mevrouw, you are kind like a mother to me. And you too, Mynheer, I thank you for paying Heer Pieterson for my schooling. I would not have liked to be a charity girl."

She ran out of the room, frightened at her own boldness.

"And that is the difference between Lysbet and Gertje," said Mynheer Varleth.

People said that the Van Der Veen house was the grandest in Niew Amsterdam. Certainly it was imposing, but not handsomer than the Stuyvesants', Lysbet thought, nor pleasanter than the Varleths'.

She soon discovered that a "cake-pasting" party was the same as the husking bees and quiltings in Wiltwyck. You came to the party and you worked, only it was much more fun to paste fancy decorations on little cakes than sewing or stripping corn.

The guests sat at long tables and at first worked steadily, but the Lockerman girls soon had the whole room laughing and playing. They had just heard that Balthazer had joined the Burgher Guard and made fun, calling him Chevalier Bayard, the perfect knight, after his illustrious ancestor. Balthazer stood for no teasing at home, but from pretty, brown-eyed Merritje Lockerman it was quite a different matter.

Lysbet sat at a side-table with Annetje Kerstedt. With them were Abram and Suusje, the Stuyvesant boys, Katryntje Van Cortlandt and little Jacob Lockerman. "The small fry," his Excellency called them as he walked about with Mynheer Van Der Veen, greeting the guests.

The children worked slowly but Annetje and Lysbet managed quite a respectable platterful of cakes. They could not help a cry of protest when Nick Bayard leaned over Suusje's head and scooped up two handfuls of their very best. He disappeared into the side entry, grinning at them. Balthazer and Nicholas Stuyvesant slipped out after him and did not come back.

"How mean!" said Annetje indignantly. "Mevrouw Van Der Veen will think we ate them." She swung around in her seat and called to her brother who stood in the hallway with some other young men, waiting impatiently for the cake pasting to be done with and the revelry to begin.

"Oh, Hans," she called, "Nick has stolen our cakes. Make him bring them back."

"You will never see those cakes again, Sis," said Hans, laughing, "but there are plenty more. It is time for supper anyway."

Mevrouw Van Der Veen was calling all the girls to help clear the tables and serve the supper, and very soon Lysbet was running about with trays filled with the Van Der Veens' rare china and glass, and plates of food.

"You are a careful one, I can see," Mynheer Van Der Veen said. "I can trust you to carry my goblets." They were beautifully etched goblets, some amber tinted, some crystal clear. Lysbet balanced the tray breathlessly. Suppose she tripped.

As she passed the table where a crowd of the older boys and girls sat, Cornelis Jansen called her. "Lysbet, stop here a moment. I want to see that glass."

He seized upon one of the goblets, examined it with the greatest care. Lysbet steadied the tray on the table as he explained to the girl next to him how it was made.

"I thought you only made window glass," said the girl, taking the goblet from him and pretending to sip.

"That is about all we do make," said Cornelis, reaching for it. "Window glass and bull's eyes, and with that my job is mostly tending the furnace. Some day, though, I hope to go to Bohemia or Italy and learn to make this kind of thing."

Lysbet was glad when the glass was back on the tray.

It was a gay supper with laughter, quips and song. Saint Nicholas' Eve came only once a year and these merry folk enjoyed it. The small fry laughed and ate as much as the others. At Katryntje's fifth cake, Abram rudely said that she might burst.

After the tables were cleared again, Old Klink, the fiddler, played for dancing. Balthazer Stuyvesant asked Lysbet to try a dance with him. Lysbet, overpowered at this honor, said she did not know how. Balthazer said that she might watch and he would ask her later.

She was unlucky, however, for Mevrouw Varleth came soon after and said the children's party was over. Lysbet was to take Suusje and Abram home and see that they went to bed. "And remember, all of you, put out your shoes for Saint Nicholas to fill. You too, Lysbet," she added, smiling.

The house was very quiet when they went in. Hans

and Joris had gone and Gertje was abed. Abram took a light from the low fire and lit a candle. The first thing was to put out the shoes on the hearth, so the Saint would see them when he came down the chimney. They covered the embers well lest he burn his toes. Then they went to bed.

Lysbet undressed in the dark and it was only as she climbed up to her own bed that she discovered Gertje's bunk was empty. Where was she? Dancing some place with her brother and his friend, most likely. Lysbet hoped she would get home before the others came and the door was barred. She was not fond of Gertje, but she did not want to see her in trouble. The Varleths, she knew, would be very angry if they caught her.

The family came home at last. There were good nights in the street as they parted from the neighbors. The boys clattered up to bed. A little later the elders followed. The watchman called eleven o'clock. Still no sign of Gertje. Lysbet lay listening and anxious.

There was a creak on the stair. The door opened softly. Lysbet sat up.

"Oh, Gertje, where have you—"

"Hush up. Ye'll wake 'em all," she shut the door. "An' if ye tell on me, I'll break your neck."

"I don't tell tales," Lysbet turned over and said no more.

Just before she got into bed Gertje spoke again. "We uns been dancing at Jock's Tavern nigh the Grove. Hans came back wi'me. We run into the Lockermans goin' home. I hid my face," Gertje snickered. "They never knowd me."

"How did you get in?" Lysbet asked.

"Cellar window under the stoop." Gertje bounced into bed.

In the morning the kloompen on the hearth were piled high with cakes and sugar-plums, presents, toys for Suusje. For Lysbet there was a wonderful surprise, a pair of skates! Not new, Mynheer Varleth told her, but an outgrown pair of Nick's, sharpened and with fresh straps. Real skates, not ox bones that most everyone at Wiltwyck had.

The Feast of Saint Nicholas, patron of Niew Amsterdam, was a holiday for everybody. The snow was gone and it had turned cold. There was hope of ice on the small ponds that studded the marsh at the Schaape Weytie.

The boys had started early but for Lysbet there were the inevitable chores before she would be free to try her skates. Feeling that she should, she asked Gertje if she wanted to come with her.

The girl, very sullen that morning, said she did not feel like skating. Lysbet heard her tell Mevrouw Varleth that Hans and Joris were already gone, that they had left Niew Amsterdam the evening before.

Free at last, Lysbet, with Suusje, started after the

others. When they reached the swamp Suusje ran ahead, joining the boys who would pull her around.

There was a maze of little streams with here and there a pond, shallow and frozen solid. Lysbet chose an empty spot for her first attempt.

She strapped on her skates and struck out. Immediately she was down. She was more cautious the next time, but even so she staggered helplessly. Someone came from behind and put a firm hand on her waist.

"Keep your feet straight and let me push you a bit. You will soon get the knack of it," said a friendly voice. It was Cornelis Jansen.

"It is so slippery," Lysbet complained, laughing.

"All you need is confidence," said Cornelis, still pushing. "Think of something else. Tell me where you learned to swim. I never saw anyone buck an undertow as you did that time in the Heere Graft. We all wondered at it."

"That was just a trick," said Lysbet, with a successful attempt to straighten one of her feet. "We used to try who could go nearest to the falls without going over. You lean backwards and the water slides under you. Little Beaver showed me."

As they stopped to rest for a moment Cornelis asked, "Who is little Beaver?"

"An Indian boy I knew. He is dead now." She was surprised to find herself speaking of Little Beaver.

"Shall we try again?" said Cornelis. Lysbet got her feet in position and they went on. Then he spoke suddenly, "Did you know, Lysbet, that the Indians killed my father and mother too?"

"Yes. Abram told me. You are just like me."

"No," said Cornelis. "I was luckier than you for I cannot remember, and the Duyckinks took me at once and treated me like their own son."

He went on. "I go up to the old place sometimes. Of course the house was burned but it wasn't much of a house, I suppose. There was an Indian village first, Sapokauican, but the poor devils left before our time and now it's called Bossem Bouwerie. There's an Englishman there now, name of Nelson. One of Cromwell's old soldiers, that came here when Cromwell died."

As they stopped again for Lysbet to get her breath he added, "It is the prettiest spot in all Manhattan. Lots of water, like this. Flowers! I have never seen such flowers in early spring. It is sort of sheltered, you know."

Then he suggested her trying to skate with him over to the others. What she needed was practice now, and more room. Lysbet took his hand and slipping and sliding she was off.

A week or two later Mynheer Varleth's rifle was missed. Nick had had it but he swore he had brought it home and put it away. They were all sure he had lost it overboard or left it on the wharf. It proved, they said, that he was not fit to have a gun of his own nor to borrow one either.

Lysbet was uncomfortable. She remembered, or thought she did, seeing three guns lying on the table with the ducks, one short and two long. She spoke to Gertje about it that night when they were alone.

The girl flew in a rage. No, she had no'seen the guns. Neither had Lysbet. If she went on saying so, they'd all be in trouble.

Lysbet was silenced for she was not really sure that she had seen three guns.

CHAPTER SIX

Secrets

❦

ALL THE GIRLS WERE MAKING MAY-BASKETS FOR THEIR
mothers and grandmothers, aunts and cousins, whoever
they admired the most. Lysbet was determined that her
basket for Mevrouw Varleth should be the most beautiful she could contrive. She would have violets, of course,
and pink trailing arbutus and something white, or perhaps blue hepatica.

Suusje wanted to make one for her step-mother too,
and they planned one together for Mevrouw Stuyvesant.
A few days before they had cut the willow shoots for the
baskets, and poked about the pastures, marking places
where the flowers grew thickest. Suusje delighted in the
jack-in-the-pulpits, "Domine Megapolensis" she dubbed
them gleefully. Lysbet was dissatisfied. She saw plenty
of violets, almost too common, but not much arbutus,
nor others she remembered in the Wiltwyck woods. It
was disappointing.

The last day of April, a precious Wednesday half
holiday, came at last. The willow baskets, lined with soft
moss, were ready, hidden in a tub in the corner of the

garden. Thanks to Suusje's efforts to keep the secret, nearly everyone knew about it, all but Mevrouw Varleth who was steadfastly deaf and blind.

Directly the noon meal was over, every girl in Niew Amsterdam set off for the woods and meadows. Lysbet was among the last, for she had to help clear the table and give a final polish to the precious pewter. Suusje, impatient, had run off with Annetje and Katryntje. Lysbet was glad, for she had her own plan. She remembered what Cornelis Jansen had said about the flowers that grew on the sheltered side of the island, beyond the Waal. Surely there she would find something rare and different for her basket.

As she started Abram joined her. The Stuyvesant cousins were still at their books, so he was at loose ends.

They went out by the Landt Poort and followed the old Indian trail, used now as a cartway. There was a marsh to the left of them on Damen's land. The cartway turned to the east and the trail went through the Lord's Waste to the west, following a brook. On the other side was a hilly pasture. "We had best stick to the path," Lysbet decided. "Then we will not get lost. I am sure there will be flowers."

They found plenty of flowers, deep purple violets, quantities of pink arbutus, anemones, white blood-root, They soon had all they needed but they went on and on, tempted by more beauty.

A great tree had fallen across the path, completely

blocking it. The up-turned root towered above them and the trunk stretched over the stream, its top resting on the opposite bank.

"We will have to climb it," Abram said, scrambling up. He peered through the tangled mass of mud and roots. "The hole is full of dirty water and it is wide. You could not jump it."

"Do not try it," Lysbet warned. "Come on down."

"We can cross to the other side," said Abram, and ran out on the tree like a squirrel.

"Come back," Lysbet shouted. "We do not want to cross."

"I cannot turn. It is too slippery." Abram landed among the branches on the other side. After a good deal of crashing about, he got clear and stood on the top of the bank.

It was not a large stream but swollen and turbulent with the spring rains, not a pleasant place for a tumble. Abram refused to come back. It was too slippery to run "back up" he said. Easy enough to come "on down."

This was true and little as she wanted to be there, Lysbet was forced to join Abram. How, she wondered, were they going to find their way over the pastures to the cartway. Abram was no help.

"I did not tell you," he said. "I hurt my knee. I can hardly walk."

"You have got to walk," said Lysbet. "I cannot carry you and we cannot stay here."

They looked around. It was uneven pasture land as far as they could see, but a foot path followed the top of the bank. "That will take us somewhere," Lysbet said wisely. "Lean on my shoulder and forget how it hurts."

Before long the path led them to a fence with a rude sort of stile.

"That is bad," said Abram. "It means loose cattle. It may be a bull pasture! I would rather face snakes with my knee like this."

"I would rather face bulls," said Lysbet. "But you stay here and I will go on till I find someone. We must be near a bouwerie, I am sure."

Abram did not like to be left but Lysbet climbed the stile. "If a bull comes from either side, you get over to the other." She looked cautiously about as she started.

Beyond the stile was a real lane turning away from the brook, and presently she came to a small stone house with sketchy out-buildings. A substantial picket fence surrounded the whole. There was no one in sight.

I will go in and ask the shortest way home, thought Lysbet. Mindful of her muddy shoes, she made for the rear door.

A dog barked furiously. She paused, glanced behind her just as a great beast bounded around the corner of the house. The watch dog! Unchained in the day time! Here was a danger worse than snakes or bulls. Terror gripped her. She rushed on.

There was a step-up side porch and a row of wooden

milk-pails drying in the sun. Lysbet caught up a milking stool and turning, swung it over her head. She let fly as the dog reached the step. It struck him on the head, checking him for an instant.

Just then the upper half of the dutch door flew open. Two strong arms seized her from behind and dragged her to safety. A man's voice shouted sternly, "Down! Down, you brute!"

The animal hurled himself against the lower door and then, obedient to command, subsided on the step.

Lysbet got her breath. Two men stood in the dim hallway. They were not young. Foreigners and gentlemen, she knew from their clothes, which though worn and shabby were of handsome cloth. She had caught the sharp command, "Down, down, you brute!" That was English.

They talked together as they led her into the kitchen and urged her to a chair. Evidently they spoke no Dutch for they questioned her with signs.

Hopefully she tried her English. "The—English—I speak. From—the—dog I to you—thanks." It was a lame effort but it brought a flood of questions that had her floundering in no time. "More slow," she begged, desperately.

They consulted together in anxious tones. Lysbet caught the words "a trap" and "call Nelson." One of the men left the room. Lysbet felt a little anxious herself. She hoped Nelson spoke Dutch.

He came hurrying across the fields at the sound of the

horn, a middle-aged, ruddy Englishman. He did speak
Dutch and it was fluent. He told Lysbet that he was the
owner of the bouwerie and saying simply that the gentlemen were his guests, he pressed her with questions about
herself, particularly what she was doing in this outlying,
desolate spot, and what she, obviously an English child,
was doing there at all.

Lysbet told him everything, from the loss of her
father and mother to the expedition for the flowers.
Nelson translated it all rapidly and added some reassur-

ing words of his own. His guests seemed satisfied. Lysbet
felt easier. She might wonder what these fine gentlemen
were doing in this outlying, desolate spot but it really
was not her affair.

Nelson said he would guide her back to the cartway,
and added that they should be off at once if she was to get
to the Poort before sundown.

Lysbet had dropped the flowers when the dog chased
her. They were scattered and trampled in the path, not
worth picking up. The great creature, friendly enough
in the presence of his master, followed them to the gate.

"I let him run," Nelson explained. "So many thieving
Indians after my chickens."

As they walked to the stile he spoke rather hesitatingly
to Lysbet. It would be a great favor, he said, if she did
not speak to anyone of his English guests. They had bitter enemies and though they had committed no crime,
still Lysbet could understand that the most innocent
man might appear guilty. She was of English birth. She
could not want their English blood upon her hands.

Lysbet certainly did not want any blood upon her
hands, like Damen. Rejoicing that Abram had not come
with her, she promised to hold her tongue.

"Just forget what you have seen and where you have
been," Nelson told her. "Have no fear. I served under
these gentlemen in old England and finer gentlemen
never drew sword in her defence."

As they approached the stile they saw Abram limping
up the lane. "What took you so long?" he shouted.

Lysbet was relieved to see him walking, but distressed to find his flowers gone. Abram did not know when he had lost them. Probably when he hurt his knee.

Nelson, a kindly man, offered a suggestion. "Jonge juffrouw, I know a place, a sunny hillside, where the wild honeysuckle blooms early. It will be in bud there now or I am much mistaken. We call it Whitsunday flower. That would fill your basket handsomely."

Lysbet looked doubtful. She did not know wild honeysuckle, but Abram raised a cheer. "Azalea! The Pinxter bloom!"

Then Nelson, by devious trails and turnings, finally brought them to the sunny slope, Abram limping at first. Just as Nelson said, there was a mass of pink and white azalea buds. Lysbet was delighted. Pinxter bloom might not make as dainty a basket as arbutus, but it would be beautiful and no other girl would have it. They gathered their arms full.

They went for a long way after that. Nelson offered to help Abram, but he said his knee was all right. They came to a good-sized brook spanned by a rough log bridge, then followed another trail.

Quite suddenly they topped a hill and were looking down at the cartway, only a stone's throw away. The hornsman was shepherding his herds toward the Poort. A group of Indians on their way out stood aside to let them pass.

"Good-bye," said Nelson. "You had best pick up your feet. Tap-toe is at hand."

"Good-bye," they shouted as they ran. Lysbet saw that Nelson had led them a merry round. She did not care. She was going to forget him and all the rest. Only before she forgot she wished she could remember where she had heard the name Nelson. She racked her brains in vain.

Next morning Lysbet and Suusje were up early arranging the baskets. After the night in water, the azalea buds had opened. Suusje was in ecstasy at their loveliness. Her own basket of purple and yellow violets was pretty but not unusual until she stuck a green "Domine Megapolensis" in the middle of it. Lysbet thought this no improvement but Suusje wanted it that way.

Lysbet had planned the presentation and instructed Suusje who promised solemnly to remember. During breakfast Lysbet would leave the table for more cream or cheese or something. She would run quickly around the house, hang the baskets on the door, do a double rap on the knocker and hide herself behind the rose-bushes. Suusje was to answer the knock and to call loudly to her step-mother to help with the heavy door. They counted on Gertje's lazy habit of letting someone else do it.

All went well at first. Lysbet thundered on the knocker and dived under the rose-bush just in time to meet Suusje diving in from the other side! They were both speechless, and Lysbet felt there was not much to be said. Now Gertje would take in the baskets!

She reckoned without the Mevrouw. It had not needed the two hurried exits from the breakfast table to give her warning. She made haste to answer that knock in person.

"Surprise! Surprise!" shouted Suusje, bursting out from the bushes, beaming with joy. Lysbet followed for her share of the pleasure.

The May-baskets were a great success. Mevrouw Varleth returned to the room with one on either arm. She could not admire them enough. The early Pinxter bloom made a great sensation.

Abram shared in that glory. He proudly described how he and Lysbet had crossed the brook and gotten lost, and how an Englishman had guided them back, and had showed them where the azalea grew.

Lysbet wished he would stop talking. She thought Mynheer Varleth looked displeased. Presently he said that though no harm had happened this time, still he did not want the children traipsing over the wastelands, getting lost and risking other dangers. Hereafter they were to stay within the Waal.

After breakfast Lysbet and Suusje set off with Mevrouw Stuyvesant's basket. They tiptoed up the path with it between them. There were plenty of places to hide in the Director's door yard, but just as Lysbet's hand was on the knocker the door flew open.

"Surprise," shouted Nicholas Stuyvesant. He and Balthazer had been watching them. They were brought in and treated to sweet cakes as forfeit for being caught. Mevrouw Stuyvesant made a great time over the Pinxter bloom.

In his office across the hall, the Director was pegging it up and down, scolding at everything: at the May Day celebrations which always led to rioting and even to bloodshed sometimes; at the English folk on Long Island who grew more and more insolent; and here had come a dispatch from Massachusetts, marked private. Trouble there, he supposed. It was written in English, and Brian Newton, his old fellow campaigner at Curaçao, now English secretary, was off on a week's trip to Fort Orange. Who was to read the silly language?

His Excellency caught sight of Lysbet and Suusje. "If that rapscallion Nick is at home," he called, "bid him come over. He at least can tell what this Endicott is after."

Nick was surprisingly good at languages, not only knowing his father's tongue French but some English. His uncle often appealed to him in small matters, but a letter from Governor Endicott was important.

Nick returned home rather puffed up. At dinner he related to the family the substance of the letter. "I could not get all the fine points," he said, "but it was asking Uncle Petrus to search for some malefactors who may be hiding here. They are the judges who signed the warrant for King Charles' death. His son, the new king, is looking for them. You can guess why." Nick made a graphic gesture across his throat.

"What makes the Governor think they are here?" asked Mynheer Varleth.

"Rumor," said Nick. "They were known to be in Massachusetts last winter. More or less looked at through the fingers, but now the hunt is on in earnest. They were last seen in New Haven in March, and it is thought likely that they are bound up the river for Canada. Uncle Petrus was willing and ready to help. He sent word to the Niew Haarlem folk to watch the road to the ferry at Spuyten Duyvil Kill and the other to Long Island. He says he will have every outgoing vessel searched."

Nick added casually. "This is all secret so that the king-killers will get no warning."

Mynheer Varleth groaned, half laughing. "Oh, Nick, we certainly are a family of secret-keepers! Remember, all of you, you have heard nothing of this state secret."

Lysbet's thoughts went tumbling over each other. The two Englishmen on the lonely bouwerie were the hunted judges! That was why Nelson had befuddled them about the way home, why the dog ran loose in the daytime; above all, why he had asked her to keep silent! Now that the search was on they would be found, taken to England to certain death. They would think she had betrayed them. "Lysbet, of the bloody hand."

Could she warn them? How? If she disobeyed Mynheer Varleth and went herself she would be missed and questioned. Suddenly, with a flash, she remembered that it was Cornelis who had spoken of Nelson, the man who had taken over the Jansen land. Cornelis would know the way. Instinctively she felt that she could trust him, but would he be willing to go? She could but try.

There was still a quantity of azalea left in the tub and Lysbet asked permission to carry an armful to Mevrouw Backer. By good management she contrived to get away without Gertje's questions. Suusje was at school. She presented the blossoms and stayed only long enough to admire little Henricus, the baby.

Behind the Backers' and across the lane was the Duyckink place, and Lysbet hoped to find Cornelis at home. She had missed him by barely ten minutes, Evert Duyckink told her. He had gone up the road to Sargeant Litscho's Tavern to deliver some new fire buckets that they had been decorating.

Lysbet had to stand while Evert gave her the story of the buckets, chuckling and drawing it out. Burgomaster Steenwyck had been hailed into court for having a sooty chimney fire. He had been fined as much as three beaver skins. Then as first Burgomaster he had ordered the money laid out in fire buckets. The Duyckinks had been given the job of painting the city arms upon them.

"The paint was still wet but what with the May Day's brawling I thought they might be needed before nightfall." Evert Duyckink laughed merrily.

"How soon will Cornelis be back?" asked Lysbet diffidently.

"You had best leave your message, jonge juffrouw.

Our day's work is over and he will be late coming home. He was going to help Burger Jorisson patch up his mill-dam 'cross the Long Island shore. What with his water-mill, and orchard, his sloop and his smithy, Jorisson has more irons in the fire than any blacksmith this side of Hades."

This was bad news. Lysbet could not leave her message so she ran on.

"The Grove is a hot spot on May Day, jonge juffrouw. No fit place for you," Duyckink called after her.

To reach Litscho's she had to pass Jochemsen's disreputable ale-house. Today the crowd overflowed the tap room, surged about the roadway and the Grove, where stood the Maypole with fluttering streamers. The dancing was over and the May Day games that his Excellency so deplored were in progress.

She pushed her way along, past the Grove and past Jock's Tavern. There she came face to face with Joris Klenck. Gertje had not said he was in town.

"What be ye doin' here," he demanded, with hardly a greeting.

"An errand," said Lysbet, trying to pass him. He turned and walked with her, asking questions, refusing to be snubbed. She saw Cornelis come out of Litscho's Tavern, down the steps. She must get rid of Joris somehow.

"Here is where my errand is," she said. "Good-bye."
"Eh, what's that?"

"I said good-bye," and she walked away.

She went quickly to Cornelis, "I have come to tell you something," she began, almost whispering. "It is about Nelson—and it is a secret."

If Cornelis had looked surprised at seeing her, he looked amazed now. "Come," he said simply, and led her around the corner of the house where the barnyard gates stood wide open. There was no one near. "What is it about Nelson?"

"You know of the two gentlemen?"

"Yes, yes. Go on." He glanced over his shoulder.

"Tell them a letter has come from Massachusetts to Mynheer Stuyvesant," Lysbet blurted out. "Tell them the North River is watched, and the ferries at Breuckelen, Spuyten Duyvil, the Niew Haarlem Road—"

"How do you know all this?" Cornelis demanded.

"I cannot tell you," Lysbet said, "but it is the truth. I do not know where they can go, but I wanted to warn them. I hoped you might help. I guessed that you—"

"You guessed right," said Cornelis. "I will go tonight. You get home as fast as you can. I can take you as far as the smithy. I must see Jorisson and the others."

They turned back into the road. It was still empty. They did not see the long foxy face of Joris Klenck pressed to the crack behind the barnyard gate, his big ears open.

CHAPTER SEVEN

Winthrop's Visit

❧

THE DIRECTOR ADDED TO HIS LARGE HOLDINGS BEYOND Kalck-Hoek Pond that spring, planned to develop the property and started to build a house.

His family, his sisters especially, were most disapproving. How could he think of taking his wife and sons to such a remote spot?

"It will not be remote when I live there," said his Excellency. Mevrouw Stuyvesant said that it would be a summer house, and that Petrus had promised to improve the Bouwerie Road.

Fredrick Phillipse, a young carpenter, helped with the plans. Dismissing weightier matters the Director rode up daily. The site must be chosen, the cellar dug, the native stone, of which it should be built, selected.

This absorbing occupation was interrupted in early July and his Excellency brought back to cares of state.

Balthazer and Nicholas Stuyvesant stepped over to the Varleths' stoop to spread the news. Their father had just received a letter from Governor Winthrop. He and his son, Fitz-John, were bound for England. They wished to sail on a Dutch ship from Niew Amsterdam.

Mynheer Varleth's eyes narrowed. He puffed a ring from his pipe. "I would wager a beaver that they are after a patent for Connecticut squatters."

"That is what Father thinks," said Balthazer, eagerly, "and that they go by way of the Netherlands to see Sir George Dowling—to get his aid with the King."

Nick called from the last step of the stoop. "I know he is English Resident at the Hague. But what have the Winthrops to do with him?"

"He is a cousin—came to Massachusetts with the old Governor," his step-father answered, "and might very well stir up some trouble now. He is ambitious for his own and not too scrupulous, no friend of ours."

Nicholas Stuyvesant broke in as Mynheer Varleth paused. "Father says we will turn out the Burgher Guard to honor Governor Winthrop."

"I fail to see why," Balthazer Stuyvesant muttered. "We know he is back of those rebels on the Long Island."

"They will be settled and Winthrop too, when the States General makes a treaty with this new King," said Mynheer Varleth, with another puff at his pipe. "When that treaty is signed our own Hartford treaty can be signed also. In the meantime it is best to have Winthrop as a friend than open foe."

The Company ship, *Niew Amsterdam,* would sail soon. Her Captain, Adriaan Blommaaert, fortunately spoke some English. The Director wrote to the Governor that it would be held for his convenience. He asked the gentlemen to stop with him during their stay in Niew Amsterdam.

The invitation was graciously accepted. Governor Winthrop and his son would come by way of Long Island and could be expected on July fifteenth.

The reception was planned. In addition to the three companies of the Burgher Guard they would have the new Cavalry Troop. Luckily some of their horses had arrived from Curaçao. There would be mounts for the visitors from his Excellency's fine stables.

A banquet was planned at the Stadt Huis with Brian Newton to translate. Nick Bayard would be also pressed into service on this occasion to talk to Fitz-John. There was an idea now that he should work at his English. Newton wished to return to England, then Nick would take over his post.

Mevrouw Stuyvesant flew about with her servants. Beds were hung out to air, her bridal linen with the Bayard crest washed and bleached, the beautiful silver polished.

"Petrus is as cross as two sticks," she reported. "It is because he fears being outwitted by that smooth Winthrop."

The fifteenth was clear and cool. Balthazer and Petrus, dressed in their Burgher Guard uniforms, rejoiced. "Think of me," said Nick, "in that Stadt Huys, listen ing to long-winded speeches, then the translations."

As both schoolmasters were in the Guard there was a holiday. Suusje had taken advantage of it to practise with her bow and arrows, and narrowly missed her father. "She wanted to shoot things at Uncle Petrus' bouwerie," she said. There was a general shout, "She might shoot Uncle Petrus."

As word had been brought to expect the arrivals at three o'clock, they gulped down their dinner. Lysbet, Suusje and Gertje would stand in the street with Abram. Mevrouw Varleth had been asked to watch from the Lockermans'.

The great ship *Niew Amsterdam* was anchored off shore. Abram, with his party pushed through crowds of porters wheeling bales of furs and tobacco from the Company's Pack-Huys to be inspected and weighed, then transferred to lighters.

Lysbet wondered, as she often had before, what it would be like to sail away and see all the places that she had learned of. Amsterdam with its great ships and canals, its Stadt Huis with the figure of Atlas bearing the world on his back, the Oude Kerk. Gertje said that all Niew Amsterdam might go inside it.

The whole town was out. Greetje, the chimney sweep, had washed his face. Handsome Thomas Pell, of Oost Dorp,* had ridden down so was dusty enough, but his

* Pelham.

coat was fine, and his demeanor proud. Abram said he had been gentleman of the bedchamber to the first King Charles, and that he, with his settlers, sitting on Dutch soil, had been made to acknowledge Dutch authority.

The Guard awaited the Governor at the ferry. They would escort him by the East River shore to the Water Poort, then take the Waal to Govert Lockerman's, picking up Hoogh and passing Burger Jorisson's, the large holdings of two Englishmen.

They would then swing down Corlear's Alley to the Stadt Huis. Most of the crowd had collected there.

Balthazer and Nicholas Stuyvesant, Jacobus Loper and plump Lucas Van Tienhoven were perched up on the stocks, which were opposite the Stadt Huis on a point which commanded a view up the river. There was also a cannon which would be fired. A lookout was to give the first hint of the arrival.

Abram joined the boys on the stocks, and Ægidius Luyck, who was standing near, took his place with the girls. He suggested going up to Hoogh Street, out of the crowd.

"But I like the crowd," said Lysbet. Suusje and Gertje liked the crowd too. It was so gay, laughing and chattering. Nobody cared a snap of the finger for this Winthrop but they loved a parade, any merry-making, and did not hesitate to show it.

After some wait the lookout shouted, "The ferry is on its way!"

The women covered their ears while the children teetered delightedly.

"Boom, boom!" went the cannon. This accomplished, there came another wait.

Their flag of white, blue and orange was wafted by the summer breeze; the arms of Niew Amsterdam, on the windows of the Stadt Huis, glistened; the sky and waters of the bay were as blue as indigo; the ships had thrown out their pennants.

All agreed that the weather was made for the day, that their city had never looked more lovely, that this important Winthrop would see now a little of their own importance.

"There! The drums, the fifes!" Smaller children were pushed forward, the boys on the stocks shouted, Gertje gave Lysbet a shove and stepped out herself. Suusje jumped into the line of march and Ægidius pulled her back.

Young Martin Cregier and Roelef Kerstedt, the drummer boys, led the way. A couple of old Company men followed them, piping lustily. Then came the first company of the Burgher Guard, flying their orange standard, led by its Captain, the popular inn keeper, Martin Cregier. Then came the second company with its blue standard. These men were younger.

Corlear's Alley was narrow and rough, but they came down it in good order, then swung the corner to the Stadt Huis.

"I see schoolmaster!" shouted Suusje. She waved wildly to attract Evert Pieterson's attention.

"Don't ye do that when our boys goes past," said Gertje, darkly. " 'Cause if ye do ye'll get well basted."

The boys, Balthazer and Petrus Bayard, were in the third company. They marched looking very brave, with their eyes straight in front of them. Stephanus Van Cortlandt had hoisted his sister Katryntje to the stocks. Like Nick he was too young to be in the Guard. Not conversant in English he had missed the greater honor, the banquet.

The Cavalry Troops, the immediate escort of the Governor, came next, struggling to keep their skittish steeds to a walk. Winthrop was under the same disadvantage but rode gallantly with a stiff inclination of his head from side to side. He was a distinguished looking man dressed in the sober garb of the Puritan. Of a good family he had been highly educated in England bι t preferred later to follow his father, first Governor of the Massachusetts colony.

It had been made evident that he wished to join the New Haven, eastern Long Island, and if possible, the Providence plantations, with his own Connecticut valley and form one great state equal in importance to proud Massachusetts. If some of his methods were questioned none doubted his devotion.

Dismounting at the Stadt Huis, he was escorted in,

followed by his son, a tall, somber-looking youth. Lysbet wondered how gay Nick would enjoy him.

The banquet, with its toasts and speeches, would take hours, so the crowd dispersed. Lysbet walked silently as Suusje and Gertje chattered of what they had seen. She was thinking about the Judges. They must have gotten away safely for they had not been caught but she had never asked Cornelis and he had never told her. She felt guilty, disloyal as to her own part in the matter and did not wish to worsen it with secret talk.

There were more grand doings that night at the Stuyvesants'. The ladies of Niew Amsterdam, debarred from the banquet, also wished to meet the guests. Mevrouw Varleth came, dressed in silk that stood alone, and Mevrouws Becker, Van Der Veen, Lockerman, Steenwyck, Van Cortlandt, Van Ruyven, De Paistre; beautiful Marie Kip, who had brought her husband, Jacob, up in the world, and other wives of prominent citizens.

The Mynheers, of lesser importance now, were also there. They made more fine speeches and Winthrop spoke in return. Translated to Dutch it made an excellent impression, filled as it was with praise of their city, their generous hospitality. He would sail the following day with real regret, he told them, for already he felt at home.

Lysbet was at school the next morning when Gertje

appeared at the door. "Heer Pieterson," she called in her
boorish way, "Mevrouw Varleth says ye must let Lysbet
go. Gov'nor Winthrop wants t'see her."

Lysbet rose to her feet in scared amazement. "Gertje,"
she stammered. "Are you sure? Me!"

"Ya," said Gertje, "Mevrouw says to change to your Church frock. Go to Mynheer Director's."

Ignoring the curious eyes of the school Lysbet put up paper and quill, wiped her fingers of ink, then followed Gertje. It was plain that she knew nothing more than what she had said.

Climbing the stairs to her room, her heart felt like lead. Had her misdoings caught up with her? What else would make the Governor wish to see her? She still felt that she had done the only possible thing but the thought of facing the Governor's and his Excellency's wrath made her quail. If they questioned her could she be silent? If not, Cornelis would get into trouble, the gentlemen may be caught.

She washed her face and hands, scrubbing at the ink. Then she dropped over her head a pretty quilted skirt and elbowed into a bodice bound with rose color. Her hair had grown and she rebraided two plaits, trying to get in all the obstinate hairs. She tied them with ribbons that she had gotten at the feast of St. Nicholas.

Gertje, who had come with her, watched sullenly. She had concluded that this affair meant new honors for Lysbet and she did not like it. If that English know'd what she knew, his smile would turn about. It was only that Lysbet knew too much about herself or she would tell.

"Ye used water an' must fetch more," she mumbled.

"Do not trouble yourself," said Lysbet, haughtily, "I will fetch more."

As they walked down the stairs Wan came in from the kitchen. She had been plucking a goose and her hands were stuck up with feathers. "Gertje say Guv'ner want you. Why for he want you?"

Lysbet, who loved Wan, longed to weep on her shoulder but could not act so with Gertje watching.

"You look pretty," said Wan, feeling her mood.

"It will take more than that, Wan," said Lysbet, smiling weakly.

As she approached the Stuyvesants' she saw them all in the summerhouse. There was Mynheer Director sitting in his favorite place where he looked out to the sea, Governor Winthrop, with his son, sat next him. The ladies Stuyvesant and Varleth sat opposite with the indispensable Brian Newton between them. There was no sign of Nick or the Stuyvesant boys and for that Lysbet was thankful. She opened the gate and walked down the path towards them with no perceptible slackening, for she must not appear frightened.

Mevrouw Varleth rose and came to meet her. "Lysbet," she said, "we have told Governor Winthrop your story and he wishes to question you. Try to talk to him in English."

Lysbet felt her heart fly from her feet to her head driving out even her few words of English. They do not know about the judges, she thought, they do not know!

"He might be able to tell us who you are," said Mevrouw Varleth, pushing her into the summerhouse. "This is Lysbet, Governor Winthrop."

"Sire, this is the girl," Brian Newton translated. "Her name must be Elizabeth, but here we call her Lysbet."

"I must have more than that to go on," said Governor Winthrop, looking at Lysbet sharply. "Since the days of our great Queen Elizabeth every other English girl child is given her name. Have you any memory of your surname or in what part of the English Provinces you lived?"

"I no remember," said Lysbet, with an instant dislike of the man. "But it was first woods. Next—river."

"You see she has even forgotten the form of her English tongue," Brian Newton broke in. "She must have been very young at the time of her capture."

"That will make it difficult to trace her," said Winthrop. "Woods and a river mean nothing. There have been so many cases of Indian outrage. She is English, that is evident, comparing her to the average stocky Dutch girl. Newton, tell Director Stuyvesant that I will make inquiries. In the meantime Mynheer Varleth can have her sent to our authorities at Hartford. On my return from England I will attend to the matter. Assuming that I do not find her people, I will get someone to take her."

Lysbet sensed his meaning and looked desperately at Mevrouw Varleth, then at the Director. What would she do if they said that she must leave them? Her father and mother were the only ones who had the right to take her and they were dead. The Varleths were her people now, by right of her love for them.

They listened attentively as Brian Newton put Winthrop's words into Dutch. Mevrouw Varleth shook her head, started to speak, but his Excellency interrupted her.

"No, no. We have taken the child in. We like her. Why should we give her to strangers? Newton, tell Winthrop this. Tell him that the girl is ours unless he can present others with a real claim."

As Newton translated, Winthrop's agreeable expression changed. "Then I must present others with a real claim," he said, stiffly. "Convey this to the Honorable Director, Newton."

Lysbet ran back to school, her heart rejoicing. Even his Excellency said he liked her.

The Governor with his son sailed on the late tide. At the last a rather strange thing happened. Into town and up to the office of Captain Van Der Grift came clattering a young Englishman, John Scott. He asked Van Der Grift, who was in charge of such matters, to procure him a sailing on the *Niew Amsterdam*.

The arrangement was just about settled when he heard that Winthrop would be on board; then he hastily withdrew his request. Taking up residence at the White Horse Tavern, he was the subject of much talk.

It was said he was also on his way to curry favor with the new King, but in a way not Winthrop's.

His father had been an officer killed in the service of the first Charles. The son had been caught later cutting the girths and bridles of one of Cromwell's troops. As a punishment he had been sent to Massachusetts as a bond-servant. At the end of his service he had gone to the Long Island, stirring up trouble in rather shady ways.

There was a rumor that he had boasted that the second Charles would give him all of Long Island in reward for his and his father's loyalty. The good people of Niew Amsterdam did not take him too seriously, but were well rid of him when he sailed on the next ship.

"Where the treacle runs, the flies gather," the Director remarked. "Winthrop, now Scott, Baxter. Each is after his own, but the three might add up for mischief."

Winthrop had let out that George Baxter was abroad, swearing that he would get back his land. He had come with the older Winthrop, but later had been the Director's first English secretary. An outrageous attempt to run up an English flag at Gravesend, unquestionably on Dutch soil, had ended his career.

The summer wore away. Bergen, the first Dutch town to the west, was chartered, and a ferry across the North River licensed. New Utrecht was founded, for not only must there be more Dutch towns on the Dutch half of

Long Island to offset the five towns dominated by the English, but more settlers were coming.

They came on every boat, substantial people, unlike those who had come at first. In a wave of hope and prosperity his Excellency built his house.

Balthazer and Petrus Bayard finished Latin School. Balthazer started business with his step-father but Petrus had an itch to wander. Nick had one more year at latin school and Abram would start. It was remarked that Evert Pieterson's discipline had done wonders for Suusje.

Lysbet had grown, and she had soaked up all the learning that was available at the primary school and would leave it that fall.

His Excellency plumed himself on her progress. He took all of the credit to himself that she had been removed from the Goosens and placed with the Varleths—also for her increasing good looks.

CHAPTER EIGHT

The Stuyvesants' Housewarming

🌷

THE STUYVESANTS GAVE A HOUSEWARMING AT THEIR bouwerie on Saint Martin's Eve. Two of the Company watchmen were to be posted at their town house else they might lose a gate or other mischief be done.

It was a family party with the Backers, Varleths and Bayards. They would start early after the midday meal. At the last minute Yoff and Wan announced that "they was goin' too, for they was skeered to stay." Abram was sent to the Director to say that the men must watch their house. The Bayard boys shut and bolted the blinds.

The Director's spiked leg made him uneasy riding, so Mevrouw Stuyvesant sat pillion with Balthazer Bayard and the other two ladies behind their husbands. One of the Stuyvesant work-carts had been piled with straw covered over with bear skins to drive the small Backers with Zoe. Now Yoff and Wan would also ride and Suusje if she got tired.

The others, with Ægidius Luyck, would walk. They followed the cart up the Heere Weg, passing the autumn cattle market on the Plain. Petrus and Cleas Vosburgh, the Stuyvesants' man, led the oxen, for not even the Lord Director's family must drive in town.

Nicholas Stuyvesant and Abram would run then leap, landing on the tail of the cart. Suusje, never to be outdone, tried it but fell ignominiously in the dust.

Nick Bayard picked her up and hoisting her to his shoulders carried her pig-a-back. He sang as he walked, an old song of evil spirits and wild huntsmen who rode on Saint Martin's Eve.

"Oh—" cried Suusje.

"They dare not come to Uncle Petrus' Bouwerie," said Nick, with a wink at Lysbet. "That is why Yoff and Wan want to go there."

Cleas got on his cart after they passed through the Landt Poort. He jounced it over the rocks and ruts accompanied by squeals, giggles and a frequent reprimand from Zoe or Wan. The four young Backers were as restless as so many squirming eels.

Cornelis Aertzen, an old man who peddled vegetables, was working in his garden just beyond the Poort. Nick Bayard yelled. "Hi, Aertzen, take care tonight!"

He dumped Suusje on the cart. "And look, Suusje, do not let Cleas drive our chariot away from us. Lysbet or Gertje may wish to hop on."

The word "Chariot" caught the ear of Nicholas Backer. "Chariot—Nick, what is chariot?"

"Chariot is a fine wagon of gold, drawn by six white

horses," said Nick. "The High Mightinesses ride in them."

"Why does not Uncle Petrus have a chariot?" Suusje yelled.

"He has this instead," said Nick, laughing.

Gertje was in one of her sulky moods and trudged in silence. Lysbet, who was walking with her, wondered if she were worried about Hans. He and Joris had appeared at Niew Amsterdam several days before, looking half starved. Mevrouw Varleth had told Wan to feed them. They would come sometimes in high feather, putting up at the questionable Jockerman's Tavern and spending lavishly. Then Gertje would be proud as a cock.

It was apparent that she was not proud or even friendly today. Lysbet fell back, joining Balthazer Stuyvesant.

Balthazer had not only grown in height that summer but had changed from a boy to a youth. He was sensitive, intensely loyal to his father and his own strong beliefs. Hearing so much of his father's talk he was developing fast, leaving Nicholas far behind him.

It had been a mild autumn. Even on the last day of October the trees were still orange and crimson. Lysbet thought of that last day of April when they were so tender green. She thought of the gentlemen and wondered where they were. Of course it was very wrong that they helped to have the King's head chopped off, but if their own were chopped off now it would not help matters.

"Two wrongs do not make a right," she had heard the Director say.

It was a balmy day with a soft haze. The low hills beyond Kalck-Hoek pond looked a misty purple. The town cattle were grazing on Lord's Waste. The yellow-weed which had lately made the ground so glorious, was dry beneath their feet.

They went down the bank at the brook, Fresh Water, that drained Kalck-Hoek to the east. There was a gourd hanging to a tree and they drank from it thirstily.

Ægidius and Nick cut poles of light willow for Nicholas and Balthazer Backer. Delighted with them they ran to the oxen. "Go, go," they shouted.

"Not without you," said Lysbet, laughing. She swung them back to the cart.

They went through the forest and up and down hill. Petrus, who carried his gun, kept it cocked, although there was little danger of hostile Indians now and most of the beasts were timid.

At a marshy pond there was a road branching off and a stone with "Two miles from the Stadt Huys." Balthazer told Lysbet that his father had put it there, and that this was their bouwerie.

They went for a couple of hundred feet and then saw the house. It was a handsome house, the second story jutting out slightly over the first. The walls were thick and the windows deep-set, for defence. There were two chimneys, one at each end, and smoke poured from them today.

As Zoe and Wan lifted off the children, the others stormed the door. "Em-m" Nick sniffed, leading the party into the kitchen. A crowd of the Stuyvesant servants were working, and on the spits forged by Burger Jorisson, a dozen or more geese, traditional to Saint Martin's Eve, sputtered and crackled.

Boofie, an old slave, was turning the spits. "Get out o' here," she cried, showing a toothless expanse of gum. "Dey's no cooked yet. You's no eat 'em now."

"If you are not careful, Boof, we will eat you," said Nick, hilariously. Then hearing voices in the room opposite, he led the way there.

It was a beautiful room, with rich furnishings which had come from Patria in the last convoy. Two of its six windows commanded a view of the river. Instead of the blue tiles about the fireplace in the usual fashion, there were panels and a mantel-shelf of finely carved wood. His Excellency, on one of his trips to the English settlements, had seen some made that way.

The ladies, having made their tour of the house, were now seated comfortably. The gentlemen were off on an inspection of the barns. The three young children must take a nap for they would sit up late. It was suggested that the others might go to the grove and gather chestnuts for the great game of the evening, Shake the Basket.

As the Bayard boys wished to see the barns, Ægidius offered to escort the nutting party. He was lent a sack for the nuts and Petrus's gun.

"I do not know if you and a gun are safer than savages and the beasts," said Mevrouw Stuyvesant, laughing.

"I do not know either," said Ægidius, laughing too.

The grove overlooked a strip of salt meadow along the river. Nicholas Stuyvesant said their father would thin it, for it cut off the view. The trees might have been saplings when Columbus came; Hudson's men may have rested in their shade. But now they must be cut by intruders who wished a view.

As the party rustled through the fallen leaves a covey of quail rose, a chipmunk ran with its young one in its mouth, a gray rabbit jumped, then was lost in a thicket.

Balthazer told Lysbet of a field mouse's nest that he had just made the reapers avoid. He hated to see defenceless creatures slaughtered.

Lysbet listened astonished. That was how little Beaver had felt.

There was a carpet of nuts in their prickly, satin-lined cradles. The young people gathered them in hand-fuls, exclaiming, cracking and munching.

"Remember the geese and the pancakes and only Saint Martin himself knows what else," Ægidius warned, but munched as much as the others. He was only twenty-two and sometimes slipped.

Gertje gave little Nicholas a slap. "Eat no more of them."

A canoe paddled by two red men slipped noiselessly past. "I can see how they might resent us here," said Balthazer, struck by a sudden thought.

"They are bad people," Balthazer Backer announced. "My father says so."

"They are not bad people," said Lysbet, thinking of Damen and his bloody hands. "Only bad sometimes, just as we are."

As the sun was falling and the sack full, Ægidius suggested that they walk back, and leave the rest of the nuts to the squirrels.

The lighted windows of the new house looked very cheerful. When all were inside, Ahasuerus, the Stuyvesant houseman, went about closing wooden blinds and bolting the doors. The two fierce and valuable dogs were untied, for who should come now could mean no good.

"Silver Peg" had kept on excellent terms with his red neighbors, and the trouble that there had been with them in the past had been none of his doings, but on this night, with its wild merry-making, someone might ignite a spark and from that a fire spread.

Aunt Judith, gay and smiling, ushered the company into the kitchen, for on this first breaking of bread all should eat together, the family at one long table; the farmer, Jacob Langestraat, with his family and some of the men at another; the help at a third.

These tables, with the stools, benches and dressers, had been made of native wood by local carpenters. His Excellency wished to stimulate home industries.

They all sat down, with a noisy scraping of new stools on the new sanded floor. Henricus Backer, the youngest, was in his mother's arms. The oldest, the Honorable Petrus Stuyvesant, sat at the head of his table. The great Bible was open before him. He read the chapter of Moses leading the Israelites to the Promised Land.

"Truly, this is a promised land," he said, visibly affected. "Flowing with milk and honey, with plenty for all. I pray that we shall be a sturdy and honorable people, mindful of God's great bounty."

His wife, who sat next him, leaned over and pressed his hand. "And, dear husband, that this shall be a happy home for us, and for those who come after us."

She was interrupted by squeals of joy from Suusje and the small Backers. Ahasuerus and Esther, his wife, were bringing on the geese. Three each, on two long trenchers surrounded by lighted candles.

Beltha Backer pointing her finger at them, tried to make her father look. He was tying her bib. "Yes, Beltha, that's for Saint Martin!"

His Excellency carved the geese at his end of the table, Mynheer Varleth at the other end. They both placed great importance on feeling the breastbones. If they were soft, the winter would be mild, if hard, severe, with ice and snow. As there were half as many geese as the months the verdict was uncertain. Hopes were divided, some wishing for an open winter, others for ice and snow.

There were heaped-up bowls of pumpkin and squash, the Virginia potato, onions and celery from Patria, conserve made from a tart red berry. For the thirsty there were flagons of sugared wine, home-brewed beer, milk and cider.

This was the first course, for the pancakes, another ritual for this feast day, would follow. The batter, light with eggs, rich with butter, was mixed and the pans were heating.

Baby Henricus, too uproarious, was removed by Zoe; the plates were passed, then passed again. "Remember the pancakes," Mevrouw Varleth called.

"Remember our walk, and the time since we've ate," said Petrus.

Boofie baked the pancakes while Wan buttered and sugared. How many of them were consumed only Saint Martin knew. Shake the Basket came next. Fingers were burned as they reached into the basket for the hot chestnuts, most of which clattered to the floor. There was a chorus of giggles and hoots and ouches. Nicholas Stuyvesant got the most and Beltha the fewest.

There was one old thing in this new room. It was a worn settle that had come from Scherpenseel in Friesland, on Grandfather Balthazer's death. The Director,

his son, sat in its corner now, relaxed and happy. He beckoned Suusje to his knee, and she, not afraid of Uncle Petrus, cuddled up affectionately.

He talked of his plans for taming new land and advised his two brothers-in-law to buy property beyond the wall. The rapidly growing city was bound to spread out. Then the Heere Weg would be extended and the Bouwerie Road improved.

"I would wish that Hartford treaty to be ratified before I buy more land," said Mynheer Varleth. "My father writes that he hears much loose talk of Connecticut's wildcat schemes."

An angry flush rose to his Excellency's cheek. "A rabble of impudent blackguards."

This was a discordant note and Mevrouw Backer hastened to divert it. "Petrus, do your elaborate plans here mean that you will never return to Patria?" This half-sister had not been in this new land so long and her voice sounded wistful.

"It means that I will not return to Curaçao," said the Director, his face relaxing. "As you know, I own a large plantation, and at one time had expected to spend my declining years there. But I find this hardier climate more to my taste. Our sons have been born here, we have dug deep in the soil. Balthazer, Nicholas, do you both agree?"

"We could not be content elsewhere," said Balthazer, "but we would like to see Amsterdam, the Hague, and other places in the old world."

"Opportunity comes with knowledge and knowledge comes through application," said his father, seizing this opening.

"Petrus! How that takes me back," Mevrouw Varleth exclaimed. "Our father was sitting just where you are sitting now, and you beside him. You both were dressed for travel, for as soon as his horse was brought he would take you to Dockum where you would go to school. 'Petrus,' he said, 'remember this. Opportunity comes with knowledge and knowledge comes through application.'"

"And it is just as true now as it was then," said the Director stoutly. "If I had followed his advice I might have preached peace in Oude Kerk at Amsterdam instead of fighting my way through life with a leg shot off." He paused, stroking his chin, his eyes far away. "I was about your age, Balthazer. Your grandfather wished me to be a pastor as he was. That was why he took me to Dockum and Latin School. There was not much learning in our small town of Scherpenseel. Most of the Friesians, his parishioners, raised cattle and the making of cheese was more important than translating odes.

"His parents lived at Dockum and I stayed with them, but unfortunately for his plans, Dockum was on the sea. A great port. I spent as much time on the water and quays as I did at my books. Those were stirring days, filled with romance and adventure. In 1576 our ten Dutch Provinces had given in to Spanish might and had been known as Spanish Netherland. The seven low Provinces had resisted and in 1609, six years before I went to Dockum, there was made a twelve-year truce between these seven and Spain which opened the sea to commerce. The great East India Company was formed in Amsterdam to trade with the Orient. Ships sailed for months and returned with fabulous treasure. Dutch merchants grew fat.

"It was a long voyage with danger from pirates and privateers. It was for that reason that their High Mightinesses sent out the ship *Half Moon* to find a western route.

"I can remember well the stir at its return. The English, Spanish and French had discovered much of the western world, but not the Dutch. There were tales of the great river, and the fortunes to be made in furs. Europe was cold and the people needed furs.

"The English had settled to the south, the French to the north. I was at Dockum when the English from Leyden settled Plymouth. Ships came to Dockum and the sailors swaggered about. They boasted of their conquests, their prizes, and of the new land where a fortune could be made for the asking. No wonder I thought a domine's life would be dull.

"At twenty-one I went to Amsterdam to enter the service of the new West India Company. The truce with Spain was over, but now the Dutch were strong too, and ready for trade and conquest. One of their admirals captured the Spanish 'Plate Fleet,' nineteen vessels loaded with a hundred and forty thousand pounds of silver! Never before had such a prize been taken."

Suusje's eyes were fixed. "What did we do with it?"

"We built more ships, to fight Spanish ships and drive them from the sea," said the Director complacently. "We had already taken much of Brazil from the Portuguese and islands in the Caribbean."

"And then you tired of a desk in Amsterdam, and went to Curaçao," said Mynheer Varleth, laughing. "One of those islands. The haunt of privateers."

"Good Dutchmen, with good ships," said his Excellency. "Some of them sent by our Company. They did much to establish our supremacy on the sea."

"And then you lost your leg," said Mevrouw Stuyvesant, leaving her place to sit next him, and leaning her head on his shoulder.

"And then I found you," he said, patting her hand, "and then came these two young rascals."

"Chips from the old block," said their mother, smiling at them.

While the talk went on, Petrus and Nick started a game of checkers. Mynheer Varleth wished that he had his chessboard. Mevrouw Stuyvesant brought out a board and beautiful set of carved ivory. One of their Captains had had them made in Cathay.

Lysbet sat with Abram and the rascals on the firebench. Her cheeks burned and she felt pleasantly drowsy. She thought of the boy at Dockum and she thought of the ships, she thought of the men who had sailed in them and settled this land. She thought of the

Indians. It was said that they had thought white men to be gods at first.

She thought of the Plate Fleet and of the Spaniards. They had taken the silver from the Indians to the south, she supposed; then the Dutch had taken it from them.

They left the bouwerie early the next morning. The Director must be at the Stadt Huis, his brothers-in-law at their desks, some of the young people at school.

It was discovered that night that someone must have broken into the Varleth house and taken a dozen boxes of shot and six of powder. The watchmen reported that they had seen or heard nothing. All the blinds were still shut and barred. How had the thieves gotten in? Only Lysbet thought of that cellar ventilator that Gertje had once used.

She thought of that missing gun. She was sure that she had seen three guns. Much as she hated it, she must have it out with Gertje. She waited until they were in their room. She would speak when she got her shoes off. Now they were off.

"Gertje—"

Gertje scowled. "What ye want now?"

"Gertje, Hans and Joris took that shot and powder. They came in that cellar window."

"Well, what if they did," said Gertje sullenly. "But if you tell on 'em, I'll tell on ye."

Lysbet was pulled up short. "You will tell what?"

"About the men at Bossem Bouwerie an' you sendin'

'em word that the Lord Director was after 'em. Joris heard all that ye an' Cornelis Jansen said. There's worse things than stealing."

Lysbet looked at her stunned. If Gertje told this, of course she, herself, must bear the blame, but Cornelis— and who besides? The word had come that all who had been responsible for the King's beheading had been drawn and quartered by this new King, his son. She had never heard that the gentlemen were safe. They might be traced even now.

"Well," asked Gertje, gruffly. "Will ye keep your mouth shut?"

"Yes," said Lysbet, climbing to her bed. She turned her face into the pillow.

CHAPTER NINE

Judith

❦

To outward appearance, the relation of Lysbet and Gertje seemed the same. For some time rooming together had been their one close contact.

Suusje, who had a room of her own now, had pleaded for Lysbet to share it. Lysbet had known that it would lead to serious trouble if she had left Gertje alone and gone down to the family floor. This she had told to Mevrouw Varleth.

She lay awake at night listening to the girl's heavy breathing. Beyond taking cakes and other things to eat, would she steal for herself, or only for Hans? Gertje loved Hans. But if she loved him she should not allow him to steal, and from those who had been so good to her and trusted her. Then Lysbet's cheeks would flame, as she remembered her own deception. The Varleths trusted her too and always talked openly before her.

The Director said that the girl was pale. She might be outgrowing her strength. Mevrouw Varleth agreed, and made it easy for Lysbet, sending her out to coast or skate with the other young people.

There was fine skating that winter and the season was long. Lysbet could hold her own now with Suusje and Annetje, but the usual Niew Netherlander, cutting curls and pigeon wings was way beyond her.

One cold, clear afternoon soon after Twelfth Night, a large party drove to Kalck-Hoek Pond in ox-sleds. With the exception of the Director, everyone went. As the moon was full they would stay late, with a special arrangement at the Poort.

"Father said that he did not care to come, but it is his leg," Balthazer Stuyvesant told Lysbet, while strapping on her skates. "But Aunt Annekin says he was once the best skater in Friesland."

"Oh," said Lysbet. "That he would have been."

Balthazer Bayard and Marritje passed them, going like the wind. Hans Kerstedt asked Jannetje, but she had promised her cousin, Stephanus Van Cortlandt. She skated away throwing Hans a coquettish smile.

The young people paired off and the older people too, Mevrouw Varleth with Domine Megapolensis, Mynheer Varleth with Elsje Van Der Veen. The children played games and tag. A crowd of men and boys lit a bonfire on the island. There was a carcass of a deer and fowls that they would roast later. The butchers played a rap-tap with their knives.

Nick Bayard was the leader in a game of Snap the Whip. Abram and Annetje shouted to Lysbet and Balthazer to join them. It was a rough game and Lysbet, at the end of a line of twenty or more, was soon snapped off, sprawling on top of fat Lucas Van Tienhoven, who was also down. With boisterous laughter he got from under, pulled her up, then went after the others.

A second crowd was playing Bull in the Ring but Gertje was with them so Lysbet decided to wait for Nick to come back. Making for the island she sat on the bank and pulled the strap of her skate tighter.

"Let me do that for you, Lysbet." It was Cornelis Jansen. He was the best skater of all the boys, but did not get away from his work very often in the daytime.

As Lysbet looked up with a bashful "thank you" it came to him how much she had changed from that day when he had seen her catch Suusje in the Heere Graft.

Her face is like a nosegay, he thought. Pink and white, that might be roses. Her eyes are blue, like gentian, that flower that we can never tame. Her hair, that might be buttercups. No, spun amber glass. That was it—spun amber glass.

"Everyone seems to be skating but you and I," he said. "Suppose we take a turn."

Joyful at this suggestion, Lysbet jumped to her feet, then clawed the air frantically.

Cornelis caught her. "Remember you are on ice," he said grinning.

Lysbet laughed. "And skates." They started off, she striking out boldly.

"You have improved," said Cornelis.

"I will do much better if the ice holds for another month," Lysbet panted. It was delightful yet terrific to skate with one of the best skaters in all Niew Amsterdam. They passed Mevrouw Stuyvesant making stately progress with solemn Mynheer Steenwyck. She called a gay greeting to Cornelis, who was a favorite.

The winter slipped by. Though the snug little city was mostly cut off from the outside world, a ship would occasionally beat its way in. An Indian might come to trade, or a settler from Wiltwyck. The word from there was, "We do not trust the Esopus tribe nor they us." The matter of the hostages was eating in. For the sake of future good feeling could they be recalled?

His Excellency blustered about, saying that this was impossible. Later he said that they might consider it in the summer when the ships came up from Curaçao.

There were the usual holidays and social gatherings, the bickerings and gossip that amused and enlivened the townsfolk. The Kips' pig had broken the De Forests' fence; someone sued someone else for debt. The Van Ruyvens' baby had had a fine christening; the Lord Director had belabored Lucas Van Tienhoven with his cane for fighting little Jacob Lockerman; Balthazer Bayard was paying decided attention to Marritje Lockerman.

Late in February there came from Hartford a startling piece of news. For the Varleths, it put even this last interesting development aside. The news came in a letter written by Tryntje, or Judith, as she was called in English Connecticut, Mynheer Varleth's last unmarried sister. She had been accused of being a witch, and was now in jail. To make matters worse, their father had died. This deplorable incident had occurred soon after New Year. She had not been able to send word earlier, the roads being impassable.

Mynheer Varleth went to his Excellency at once, and they both conferred with the Domine. There was no doubt of the seriousness of this charge. Judith's brother should go at once to Hartford and move heaven and earth to get her freed. The Director, connected to her by close family ties, would write a strong letter.

There were few boats sailing as yet. Mynheer Varleth must ride. He would go by way of Niew Haarlem and Oost Dorpe, then on to New Haven and from there to Hartford. The faithful Brian Newton would go with him as interpreter.

They must take food for the trip and trust to luck in changing their horses. Both men had gone the way often, but never in this season.

After they left, Mevrouw Varleth waited in great suspense. Finally a letter arrived, brought by an English coastwise ship. Judith had been cleared of the ridiculous charge and they were starting for Niew Amsterdam at once. They would travel by horse and might be expected soon.

The ship had also brought Judith's possessions. Two great chests and innumerable pieces of furniture. "What shall I do with them all?" said Mevrouw Varleth. "What shall I do with Judith?" A girl who had been accused of witchcraft!

Seldom had the town had so juicy a topic. As a culmination, Domine Megapolensis preached a sermon on witches. Summing up the case he had said, "The apparition of a person afflicting another is a very insufficient proof of a witch. A good name obtained by a good life should not be lost by mere spectral accusation."

That settled the matter with some. Opinion varied with others, Nick Bayard declaring that of course Judith was a witch. She had a hook nose, a hump on her back, and rode on a broom.

"Nonsense," said Mevrouw Varleth. "Judith is only seventeen and a beauty."

Abram backed up his step-mother. He had seen Aunt Judith after his mother had died and she was not a witch.

"Ha, ha," said Nick. "To fool one is part of their witchery."

Soon after the letter, and in early evening, the party arrived. Judith had ridden behind her brother, and was so stiff she must be lifted down.

"The poor child had been sitting from six in the morn till seven at night," said Brian Newton.

Judith laughed, stamped her feet to bring back the feeling, then turned quickly to throw herself into Mevrouw Varleth's arms. She was a small figure looking almost as broad as she was long in her heavy furs.

The mistress had gone out by way of the sacred front door. For this special guest the "threshold covenant" should be observed. Suusje had also slipped out and was patting Prince Maurice, her father's big horse, while the Bayard boys were taking the saddlebags from the packhorses.

Lysbet, in the kitchen, was desperately trying to straighten it. She and Gertje had been sewing on patchwork and there were scraps on the floor. She gathered them up, pushed back a basket of pieces, and set the chairs right.

The dishes from their supper were still on the table; they were Gertje's chore. She was probably peeking from the alleyway, Lysbet thought. But there was no time to clear them. Mevrouw Varleth, with her guest, had stepped over the threshold now, and they were coming along the entrance hall. As Judith was ushered in Lysbet hesitated, then stepped forward a little shyly.

"Judith, this is Lysbet," said Mevrouw Varleth, smiling at her. "I expect you have heard about Lysbet."

"Oh, yes!" Lysbet caught a glimpse of dimples. She helped divest Judith of her wrappings, a great coat of beaver, and under that two thick jackets of wool. As they were pulled off Judith went into peals of laughter, in which Lysbet could not help joining. Judith pulled up her petticoats, blue, ash color, green, to show them. "I carry all my clothes on my back," she giggled.

Starting to take off the top one, she noticed Nick, who was entering with one of the saddlebags, and gave a little squeal.

"Nick, if those are Judith's extra things, we will take them to her room," said his mother, with dignity. "Judith, you will sleep with Suusje. I hope that you will not mind."

As they went up the corner stairs Mynheer Varleth and Brian Newton were swept in by an uproarious escort. Suusje on Newton's shoulder, Abram, Petrus and Balthazer Bayard loaded with more saddlebags, the Stuyvesant boys, who had seen the arrival and had run over, crazy to see a witch.

Gertje, who had sneaked in by the back door, was clearing the table, setting fresh places for the travelers. Wan, in her domain, was building up a fire, splitting a shad for their supper.

Suusje plumped herself on Brian Newton's knees and tried to tickle his neck. Abram told her not to make herself a nuisance. Petrus pulled off his step-father's boots and brought him house-slippers, while Balthazer put away the brace of pistols which he had carried in his holster.

They had been fired twice, once to scare a wildcat, the second time to pepper a pack of wolves, bold from hunger.

The Stuyvesants, sitting on one of the settles, openly stared when Judith came back. Peeled down to the usual

number of garments she was slender but with a round-
ness that suggested a kissable baby. A blonde, as were
most of the Dutch girls, she had a dazzling complexion
and a bewitching smile. She smiled with her eyes and
her mouth and her dimples, twinkling all over.

She talked as she ate, delighting Suusje, Lysbet and
the boys. The frightening experience of having been
imprisoned as a witch had apparently made no impression on her volatile mind. She rattled on describing the
muddy trails, the vast distances between the settlements,
the wolves which had followed them, scaring her out of
what poor wits she had. Finally, to everyone's astonish-
ment, she started to laugh, then burst into tears.

Mevrouw Varleth tried to soothe her but finding it
impossible, lit her candle and marched her off to bed.
Judith, without doubt, was highly overwrought from
what she had been through, and from the three days'
hard going, dead tired.

With her safely in bed Mynheer Varleth told the story
which they had been impatiently waiting for. Judith
had been accused by an English girl, Anne Cole. This
girl had been subject to spasms in her childhood and
lately they had gotten worse. She jabbered in Dutch, a
tongue supposed to be foreign to her, but which she
could have picked up. She declared that Judith had
bewitched her.

"But how could she have been believed?" asked Mevrouw Varleth, indignantly.

"There is great superstition about," said Mynheer Varleth. "Then our father had left much property and if Judith had been proved guilty that would have been taken." He added, "Balthazer, Nicholas, it was your father's letter which helped me most. Tell him that we will visit him tomorrow to thank him."

As the month wore on, it became plain that Judith was a witch for she charmed everybody, at home and abroad. She was gay, good-humored, and if a bit light-minded that was natural to her age. Her clothes, bursting from the chests, were of the best style and quality. Her father had been a man of consequence, not bound by Puritan laws.

The impressionable Nick was her first victim, a distraction at this time. The post for which he had been working had come his way. Brian Newton was really going, and Nick, just out of Latin School, would take his place.

"He was riding to position on top of the family wheelbarrow," some were mean enough to say. Others said that the lad, with his French and English, deserved the honor.

With the varied population the records were kept in three languages, as were the placards that were posted in the town. Letters must be written and read, bills of lading made out in French and English.

As Nick's English was shaky he appealed to Judith. She had lived among the English and spoke it well. She explained, pointing out errors, "You form your sentences as if they were Dutch. Remember, this is English."

Lysbet listened. Long forgotten words came back and she learned new ones. Her tongue did not have the trouble that poor Nick's had. "It is a marvel how fast she picks it up," Judith declared. Nick thought it a marvel too.

Judith stayed till late June, then went down to De-la-warr to visit a sister, Mevrouw Heermans. Augustine Heermans, her husband, was coming up on business, and would take Judith down. He had been one of the first citizens of Niew Amsterdam, but having mapped Virginia and Maryland for the English, had been given an enormous grant of land. He called it Bohemia Manor, and had moved his reluctant wife down there.

It was hoped that Judith would return, so she left most of her things. The furniture was hauled up to the peak of the house and stored away securely. Repacking the chests, she picked out a doll that had been hers for Suusje, an embroidered collar and apron for Gertje; then looked over her jewelry to find something really nice for Lysbet.

She decided on a pin with a blue stone; then, struck by a sudden thought, looked for her gold beads, one of the last gifts of her father.

Not seeing them she went to the bottom of the chest, pitching things out. Then she replaced everything in the chest, shaking each one. Could Suusje have taken them to play with? Suusje had taken a violent interest in all her things, but so had Lysbet and Gertje. She left the doll on the top and with it the small quilted petticoats, tiny jackets trimmed with bits of lace and gold braid, that she had made as a child.

She asked Suusje about the beads that night. "Had she played with them and forgotten to put them back?"

"Oh, no," said Suusje, "I would not go to your chest, Aunt Judith." Then she added, "I have gold beads too, and pins and bracelets and a chatelaine with everything on it. They belonged to my real mother. Father will give them to me when I reach sixteen."

"Then I left my beads at Hartford," said Judith. She took out the doll. "Suusje, I had thought to save her for my own little girl, but she does not want to be buried for years in a chest."

Speechless with pleasure, Suusje hugged the doll. "I will call her Judith."

Judith looked at the pin, then at the collar and apron. Hesitating a moment, she put them back in the chest and closed it. Yoff would strap it on the morrow and wheel it to the wharf. There would also be Petrus' baggage, for taking advantage of the opportunity, he was going too.

Nick spoke at the moment of parting, before everyone, publicly. He would be nineteen on his next birthday. He was Clerk of the Council, English and French Secretary; on the way to fortune. He did not care who heard him say that he adored Judith, for they all knew anyway.

His mother stood aghast. Judith giggled, at the same time blushing furiously. "In all my life, Nicholas Bayard! Why not publish it by the town crier?"

"I will if you dare me to," said Nick.

"If you dare me, back you go to swaddling clothes," said his mother. "My fine young man, wait till your brothers step off before you talk of adoring anybody—"

"That is it," said Nick. "Petrus stepping off with Judith now, and down to the wilderness where there is no one else but savages."

"Do not worry yourself," said Petrus. "If I had wanted to make love to Judith I'd have tried before and not stepped aside for you."

His Excellency settled the question. "In the course of time it might be a matter to consider, assuming that Judith is favorably inclined."

Judith showed her dimples. "Nick, dear Nick, work on your English or else we may starve."

The loss of Judith's beads had made no impression on Suusje's mind. Summer was at hand with all its distractions and delights. She was taken out of school during the hot months and she, with Abram and Lysbet, made a long visit to the bouwerie. The Stuyvesants had gone up to plant the flower gardens and beautify the place generally. There was a small village now for the laborers, a chapel for their worship. Domine Selwyn, the pastor at Breuckelen, rowed over every Sunday afternoon for a service.

Philip Schuyler had started his new settlement near Wiltwyck and there was definite hope that the hostages would be traced and some of them returned. Then the Esopus tribe might be pacified.

In August the Governor of Nova Scotia arrived in Niew Amsterdam, with three delegates from Boston, to plead for Director Stuyvesant's aid. The Mohawks were raiding settlements on the Penobscot River.

His Excellency, complaisant, took them to Fort Orange to meet the Sachems. Nick, highly delighted, went with them as English interpreter.

He confided to his step-father, on his return, that one of the delegates had told him that Winthrop's friendship could not be trusted, that he had no love for the Dutch, calling them "our noxious neighbors." He undoubtedly wished to absorb the Dutch half of Long Island and as much more as he could get.

Nick had not dared to repeat this to his uncle. He had thought in this instance of the old Dutch proverb, "speech is silver, silence gold."

Mynheer Varleth looked serious. "It is your duty to tell him everything that you hear. A word here, a word there are like drops in a torrent that may in time engulf us if we are not prepared. But grit your teeth and hold on to your head," he added with a wry smile. "Your uncle will not like 'noxious neighbors.'"

CHAPTER TEN

Unexpected Meetings

OCTOBER BROUGHT THE CATTLE FAIR. THE MARCKTVELD and all the neighboring byways were crowded with men and animals. Cattle-pens and hitching-posts extended far up the Heere Weg to the Burying Ground and beyond. Cregier's Tavern at the corner of the 'Veld did a thriving trade. Here gathered the cattle-men from up the River, from Niew Haarlem and Oost Dorp and the sheep-drovers from distant Connecticut farms.

The morning breeze was off shore and the lower town suffered. In spite of the stench, Perel Street was gay with stalls offering trinkets, knickknacks, woodenware and all manner of cakes and pasties. The water-front was lined with market boats from the small bouweries of the Long Island and from Bergen, the new settlement across the North River.

Wandering Indians peddled birch-bark baskets. Jugglers performed. A swarthy sailor, newly arrived from Curaçao, carried a cage full of talking parrots. Another rough fellow led a shaggy bear by a chain. The beast could dance, he said, and claimed they came from Canada, an unlikely story.

Fair time made small difference to the great folk of Niew Amsterdam. Mostly they stayed within doors. Mynheer Varleth's household was occupied with the great wash. Wan had scalded her wrist a month back and it had been long healing. The wash had been put off and now as the days grew short, there was no time to lose.

Wan and Gertje set out early for the Maagde Paetje,* a stream just beyond the Water Poort on Waal Road. Yoff went with them to trundle the barrow which was heavy with the contents of Mevrouw Varleth's great linen chest.

Lysbet was kept back to help the Mevrouw tidy the house. Afterwards she was to join Wan and Gertje and bring lunch for the three of them. The Mevrouw sent her off with many directions.

"I am trusting to you, Lysbet, to look after things. Wan understands the washing but she can not count, and Gertje is unreliable. Try to keep the sets together as you pack them, and count them all. Be inside the Poort by sundown and wait in front of Litscho's Tavern till Yoff comes." Then she gave Lysbet money to buy Kirmis pasties for them all.

Lysbet threaded her way through the crowd, delighted to see the fair at close hand. She chose the pasties with care, juicy ones cased with mustard and sugar and wrapped in cabbage leaves. There was money left for a round of oil fritters and some batter cakes, none of them

* Maiden Lane.

so good as Wan cooked at home but this was Kirmis food.

As she turned from the booth a tall man stepped in front of her. "Good morning, jonge juffrouw. I have been on the watch for you."

Lysbet looked up, startled until she recognised him. It was Nelson, the Englishman of the Bossem Bouwerie. It was all of a year and a half since her encounter with him.

"There is a man here from Connecticut, come down with some sheep. He has a message for you," Nelson explained. "Follow me at a little distance. We do not want to make trouble for you. He is over near the well on the Marcktveld." Nelson strolled off and after a moment Lysbet followed him.

She had no doubt this message concerned the two fugitive judges. At last she was to hear what had happened to them. She crossed to the well, set down her basket and drew the bucket towards her.

Nelson was standing nearby, in conversation with another tall fellow in a drover's smock. He turned to her.

"This is the man, jonge juffrouw. Sperry is his name. He speaks no Dutch but I will translate if you wish."

"I speak more English than I did but I do not always understand," Lysbet said. "It will be quicker if you tell me what he says."

It was a message from the two English gentlemen, as she had thought. First, before all, they thanked her for the timely warning which had undoubtedly saved their lives. Providence and kind friends had led them through many dangers to a haven far away where they were as safe as they could ever be while a Stuart reigned in England.

Now for the message. They had learned the details of Lysbet's story from the young man who had aided their escape that night. In their wanderings on the borders of the wilderness they talked to many people. They would inquire and question constantly. In time they might happen on some clue to her identity. Already they had one lead. Did the word Cloomber mean anything to her? Had she heard it before? Cloomber?

Lysbet shook her head. It meant nothing to her. "Is it the name of a flower," she asked, guessing wildly—"a purple flower like a lilac only a very different smell? It is a smell that reminds me of something, I do not know what."

"You are thinking of lavender," Nelson said, "sweet lavender. That would be common in any English settlement. It has nothing to do with Cloomber."

Lysbet was sorry she could be of no help. She could only thank Sperry for his message and send greetings to the judges in return. She was glad to learn of their safety and grateful for their efforts in her behalf. She said goodbye and hurried away to join Wan and Gertje at the washing stream.

Beaver was the street nearest the well and she sped along it, her cheeks flushed, her eyes shining. What mattered her own worries now that the judges were really safe. She was glad to learn at last that they were at such a great distance from Niew Amsterdam. She thought of Gertje and wondered if this word from the judges now made a difference. But Gertje was not stealing, she was sure, and there was still Cornelis and the "others" he had spoken of.

Was it all on their account that she had yielded to Gertje's threat, or despicable fear for herself? She hoped not but did not know.

Her thoughts wandered on. "Cloomber?" What did they mean by Cloomber, and what might she have remembered? Would the judges, in their searching, find someone with a real claim? Then should she have to go? To Hartford, maybe, into the jaws of Winthrop.

Outside the Water Poort was the country. The houses were low with thatched roofs, and the air smelled fresh and sweet. Lysbet wrinkled her nose at the thought of the cattle-market. The lane that ran along the washing stream was choked with yellow-weed and purple daisies. The pools were deserted. The Varleths had the place to themselves in market time.

She found Wan and Gertje well up the stream, hard at work. The first washing was already spread on the grass and a second lot was boiling in the great iron kettle that the Varleths shared with the Stuyvesants and Backers.

As soon as Lysbet arrived Wan said it was time to eat. They sat on the grass while she unpacked the basket. She showed them the Kirmis cakes and regaled them with the sights of the market-fair, the jugglers, and the clumsy dancing bear, and the cage of chattering parrots. Wan listened grinning and at first Gertje stared, astonished, at Lysbet's unusual friendliness. Lysbet went on to tell how old Widow Geveret had bought a suckling pig and let it slip on Brower Street hill. Before it was caught, it had upset the tray of a ginger-bread vender, careened against the stout legs of the Widow Geveret and tumbled her into the dust and the ginger-bread.

Suddenly Gertje shouted with laughter, slapped her sides, and rolled over on her back, kicking her legs about. It was the kind of joke she understood. She sat up and began talking uproariously.

Wan, who had been dozing over her last Kirmis cake, woke suddenly and declared that they must get back to work. They finished in good time and as they folded and packed the pieces, Lysbet tried inconspicuously to count, until she saw the others were at it too. Wan, neither reading nor counting, had a system of her own that apparently added up right, and Gertje made no secret about it, numbering the pieces in a loud whisper. In silence they tied the cover-cloth over the load.

It was down hill from the washing ground to Waal Road and the barrow ran easily. Wan limped after them. She had done a hard day's work and was tired. She sank down comfortably on the steps of Sergeant Litscho's Tavern and was asleep before the girls had hauled the barrow to the side of the road.

There was a half-hour to sundown when Yoff was
due. Lysbet and Gertje strolled down the road in search
of amusement. The tavern yards were filled with carts
whose owners still lingered on the Marcktveld driving
last-minute bargains.

As usual something was going on at the Grove. Two

men were wrestling for a money prize, offered by the wily taverner, Jochemsen, who more than doubled his outlay from thirsty spectators.

The girls were in time to see the last of the fight. The winner was a stocky young man in the early twenties. He had squinty eyes and a mop of sun-bleached hair. Lysbet felt that she knew him but she could not think who he was. As she stood wondering, someone moved behind her and two greasy hands came over her eyes. A rude voice spoke in her ear, "Guess who's got ye?"

She knew then. It was that hateful Dirck Goosen from Wiltwyck, and the squint-eyed young man was his brother, Jon. Lysbet twisted herself out of his grasp and stood scowling at him. All her old hatred rose within her.

"I thought as maybe ya'd be glad ter see me, Lys, see-in'aa I been like a brother to ya, but ya ain't changed a mite."

"No, I have not changed," Lysbet said shortly. "What do you want, anyway?"

"Naught from you, High Mightiness. Me and Jon have quit Wiltwyck for good an' all. We've took up land in Bergen 'cross the river, raisin' chickens. What we want now is a wife to cook for us an' look after the hens." He winked at Gertje who stood gaping.

Jon had come up and was counting his money. He had never been as bad as Dirck and Lysbet spoke to him. He grinned back but his eyes were intent on Gertje.

Dirck broke in, "Who's that girl? She ain't bad lookin'."

"Come, Gertje, we must get back to Wan," said Lysbet, for this was a little too much.

"Naw," said Gertje. "I be in no hurry. My name's Gertje Kolp," she added with a giggle and glance at Jon.

Lysbet walked off. She was annoyed but after all, why should she care if Gertje wanted to talk to Jon Goosen. He was not very bright and followed his brother slavishly. But he was honest and much better than that Joris Klenck, or even Gertje's own brother. They were thieves, and to make it worse they had most probably traded the gun, powder and shot to the Indians, a crime in itself.

Supper was late that evening, but it was ready and waiting before Mynheer Varleth and Nick came in. They had been with his Excellency the whole afternoon and looked jaded.

"Your brother grows more irascible every day," Mynheer Varleth told his wife. "In this case I do not blame him. No one can see what Winthrop is about. It seems that he has obtained his charter. It makes the most impossible claims as to boundaries, ignoring our very existence, as well as the wishes of the English New Haven colony and the Providence Plantations, which do not intend to be swallowed by Connecticut.

"This charter was published in Hartford some time ago with fanfare and shouting, but had only today come to the Director's hand, and will cause a peck of trouble before it is straightened out."

"I do not wonder that Petrus is wild," said Mevrouw Varleth, who realized the seriousness of this news. "What with the niggardly Company, who, notwithstanding everything, he is so loyal to, the States General, who want to keep peace at home, and this new king and his Dowling."

"There are rumors that the Company is not quite so opulent as it was and that their High Mightinesses may take us over, lock, stock and barrel."

"They had better do it quickly," said Mevrouw Varleth, "else we may fall disastrously between the two." She turned to Nick. "And where have you been dallying, Nicky Bayard, with your supper ready and Wan and Gertje, dog-tired, longing for their beds. Settling this whole matter, I make no doubt."

"I was writing a letter," Nick began, but Mynheer Varleth interrupted. "Mynheer Bayard, the Secretary of the great West India Company has spent the afternoon transcribing a sharp letter to our neighbor, the worshipful Governor of Connecticut."

"Yes," said Nick, gloomily, "and every time I got started, Uncle Petrus would think of another way of saying it. I finally got it all down in plain English that will warm the Governor's ears."

"If you got down a half of what your Uncle said, his ears and eyes too will be burned to a crisp," said Mynheer Varleth cheerfully.

CHAPTER ELEVEN

Nick Bayard's Pen-knife

❦

THE COMPANY'S SHIP, *Gilded Beaver,* HAD BROUGHT other livestock along with the talking parrots. There was a final shipment of horses, ordered from Curaçao, for the cavalry troop intended for the protection of the Long Island. The scheme had proved impractical, and after displaying their very showy uniforms in a few parades, the troop had quietly disbanded.

His Excellency was saddled with the disposal of the horses. "Truly," he complained, "the duties of a Lord Director are varied. Never did I think to be a horse trader."

Still another form of livestock arrived on the *Gilded Beaver,* two of the Indian captives so regrettably sold into slavery. The Director had been working for months to recover them, both to soothe the feelings of the proud Esopus Nation and to ease his own Dutch conscience. These two were all that could be traced and redeemed.

In Niew Amsterdam they were given presents, feasted and dispatched up the river to their own people. But it was too late to mend matters, for the Esopus tribesmen were discontented and suspicious. The new white settlements encroached alarmingly on their planting lands. They watched from their villages, muttered and bided their time.

In Niew Amsterdam the folk prepared for the approaching winter. Roofs were repaired, storm windows made tight, woodpiles replenished. Before freezing weather set in Petrus Bayard returned from De-la-warr.

Naturally quiet, he had little to say about his visit. Yes, Bohemia Manor, the Heermans' estate, was beautiful, and enormous. His uncle Augustine was experimenting with various plants, tobacco and indigo, and medicinal herbs. Petrus did not know how successfully. Yes, he had enjoyed his visit but it was too lonely. Judith, he knew, felt the same. She had wanted to come back with him but had doubted her welcome.

"Oh dear," groaned Mevrouw Varleth, "if it were not for Nick's foolishness, there is nothing I would like more than to have her live with us."

Poor Nick! He wished his impulsive words unsaid, offered to cut out his tongue if ever he said such things again. He promised and begged until his exasperated mother agreed to write Judith and suggest her coming to them in the spring. It was only that the boy was so young, and that objection would in time remove itself.

In the spring the long-feared blow fell. The Esopus Nation took the war-path. The first news to reach Niew Amsterdam was the arrival of several boat loads of refugees from Wiltwyck who came paddling down the river with the tale of blood and horror. The new Schuyler settlement had been wiped out, not a house left standing, seventy persons killed, many more taken captives. The savages, mad with war-lust, were sweeping onward. Ensign Dirck Smit, holding the block-house at Wiltwyck, sent frantic pleas for help.

Hans and Joris had come down with a canoe full of women and children. They tied up at the town wharf and lingered, hoping to get a return load of vengeful fighting men. Hans stepped over to the Varleths' kitchen to give an account. Lysbet shuddered when she heard it. She knew what it meant to be cooped up in the Wiltwyck block-house.

The Director and his Council conferred together, while the townsfolk stood around the streets with anxious faces. Balthazer Bayard and Hans Kerstedt with young Martin Cregier and his drum, marched about enlisting men and boys to go immediately to the relief of Wiltwyck. Half a dozen lusty fellows had fallen in behind them.

As the party approached the wharf, Hans spotted Joris Klink taking his ease in the canoe. "Here is a prospect," he called out.

"I know him better than you, "Balthazer said. "I will lay you two to one we do not hook him."

"Done," said Hans. "What shall it be? Guilders?"

"Guilders? No, let's say stivers, and have it for keeps.

Make music on your drum, Martin. Wake the fellow up."

Hans lost the bet, for despite the thundering drum, Joris slept soundly until the party moved on. One of the new recruits lagged behind. He leaned over the canoe and just as the sleeper opened one cautious eye, he shouted a war-whoop, then ran off mocking. It was Cornelis Jansen, who had been one of the first to volunteer. He had a debt to settle with the Redskins.

Meanwhile the Director and the Council acted promptly. Half the garrison of the fort was dispatched up the river. For the next two weeks every effort was made to raise men. The older settlers, who remembered former Indian uprisings, came forward, however unwillingly. More recent colonists protested. They had been promised protection and saw no reason to leave their homes and go miles away into the interior fighting the Company's battle.

The Authorities offered bounties, tax exemptions, promised pensions and free plunder. By these means a respectable force was gathered and after a hasty training they, too, were sent up the river under the able leadership of Captain Martin Cregier.

It was a bitter day for Nicholas Bayard when his two brothers set off for the war. His inflated position no longer pleased him.

"If I am old enough to write, I am old enough to fight," he said.

As Nick had been a bit boastful, Balthazer could not resist, "Perhaps you would fight no better than you can write, Nicky. We hear rumors that Governor Winthrop never answered that letter because he could not understand your English." Whether true or not, the taunt made Nick furious. He slammed out of the room without saying good-bye.

Later, on the wharf as the Guards were embarking, Nick came running to shake his brother's hand. As a parting gift, he brought his silver-handled penknife, a prize he had won for penmanship at school, a treasured possession. Balthazer would not take the knife but they parted the best of friends.

All the girls had turned out to bid the boys Godspeed. The Lockermans, Annetje Kerstedt and several others were making a great time and half in earnest, weeping over each lad who came along. English Lysbet, standing a little apart with Suusje, marveled at such unrestraint. Cornelis Jansen came over to her. He was laughing and straightening his collar.

"I have just been making the round," he said. "I did not know what was going on until Stephanus told me." Cornelis stopped laughing and spoke seriously. "I wanted to tell you, Lysbet, I am going into this fight to settle my own private account and I will give a few extra blows for you."

Lysbet smiled at him cheerfully though she did not feel so.

"Good-bye," she said. "Do not get killed."

"Not if I can help it," he said. "Good-bye, Lysbet. Good-bye, Suusje."

Why must there always be fighting, Lysbet wondered. She did not feel vengeful towards the Indians, not when she thought of Little Beaver.

The boys were gone at last amid cheers and waving kerchiefs. The town folks settled again to humdrum affairs. Not so his Excellency. For him difficulties loomed on every hand. Foremost was the sore question of the Connecticut boundary line, and the unjustifiable claims of the new Charter. The English group, under Pell, had perforce accepted Dutch authority at Oost Dorp. The Connecticut Charter was upsetting them, it was said, laying claim to all that region.

Ready to try all peaceable means of arrangement, his Excellency got on his barge and himself made a trip to Boston to put the whole matter before Governor Endi-cott and the Federal Commissioners. He returned dis-satisfied, for the Commissioners had pointed out that as long as Governor Winthrop remained in England, no permanent decision could be made. This much they yielded: for the space of one year matters should remain in *status quo*. His Excellency was disturbed. What was to follow that one short year?

Since peace had been declared between the English and Dutch homelands, the Director's hands were tied. His appeals to the West India Company for aid and instruction brought counsels of appeasement. Give no cause for offence, they wrote, but fortify the harbour and be prepared to defend yourselves.

Causes of complaint continued to grow. A Dutch salt-maker at Gravesend was set upon by his English neighbors, beaten and run out of town. His plant was burned, but when called to book, the local authorities flouted the Director's orders and insolently ran up the English flag.

Hearing of Winthrop's return to Connecticut, Director Stuyvesant determined to try another remonstrance. He summoned Secretary Van Ruyven and together they composed a letter, pleasant, reasonable, no cause for offence but steadfast and determined.

This letter was handed to poor Nick to translate. Even in Dutch the matter was involved, and his brother's jeers had shaken his self-confidence. He was ready to ask help from anyone. If only Judith were there! His mother had written as she had promised and Judith was expected any day now, but that did not help. Then he remembered Lysbet and that Judith had praised her English.

"I will take it home with me, Uncle Petrus," he said, gathering up the papers. "I will bring it back in a couple of days."

"A couple of days!" exclaimed the Director. "Bring it back tonight. I will sign and seal it. Send it tomorrow morning."

Nick took his way to the vine-covered summerhouse

at the bottom of the garden, shouting as he passed the windows for Lysbet to bring him his lap-desk.

He explained what he wanted when she came lugging the little desk. "I mean for you to check the spelling, and polish it, you know."

Lysbet was ready to help him as much as she could. She made a trip to the house for the dictionary while he prepared the quills with his knife. Suusje came running, curious as usual. Nick ordered her off and together he and Lysbet grappled with the problem. It ended with Lysbet thinking up the words and Nick writing them down in his beautiful copper-plate hand.

When it was finished he read it aloud and they agreed that it sounded like very dignified English. Lysbet thought some of the sentences too long.

"This one, for example," she said, reading. " 'Nevertheless as peace union and neighborhood ought to prevail between Christians in these wildernesses under so great multitude of barbarians Indians living.' Do you see what I mean? Is it clear?"

"It seems clear enough to me," Nick argued, "and if I can understand it, surely a real Englishman should have no trouble."

The translation had taken them the whole afternoon. They had been too busy to notice a small sailboat tacking slowly up the harbour. The first they knew of Judith's coming was her appearance at the front gate,

wreathed in smiles and followed by a couple of seamen
carrying her chest.

Nicholas leaped to his feet. "It's Judith!" he shouted.
"You take the letter to Uncle Petrus, will you, Lysbet?
Hey, Judith!" He was gone.

Lysbet raced over to the Stuyvesant house. The study
door was open and the Director was seated at his table,
looking over some mail and making growling noises in
his throat. He nodded briefly and motioned her to put

the letter down and go. He was in a rage, and at the boil-
ing-over point, Lysbet thought as she skipped out. "I
wonder what about." Then she forgot him in her pleasure at Judith's return.

She was greeted heartily when she came in.

"I am glad you are still here," Judith said to her. "I
was not prepared for Balthazer and Petrus to be gone.
Bohemia Manor is so far from everywhere, we had no
idea that this Indian war was so bad, but now I hear the
danger is over. That is the way to be told bad news, the
happy ending first—"

Mynheer Varleth caught up with her. "The danger
over? You heard nothing of the kind! I said the city was
safe but the war is by no means over. Another spring
will perhaps see the end of it."

Light-hearted Judith paid no heed. She was happy
and wanted the others to be so too. Her high spirits
affected them all and the evening was the pleasantest
that they had spent since the boys had gone.

Even the sullen Gertje shared the general good-
humor. She talked to Lysbet that night as they undressed, complaining, but not as disagreeably as usual.
It was easy, she said, for Judith to look pretty with her
fine clothes and no hard work to soil her hands.

"Well, there is nothing to stop us washing our hands
if we want to," Lysbet laughed as she scrambled up to
her bunk. She was asleep before Gertje blew out the
candle.

Hours later Lysbet was roused by a creaking in the bunk below. The room was flooded by moonlight, bright as day. She leaned over and looked down. Gertje was sitting up, examining something in her hand. Lysbet started to speak and stopped for she saw what the thing was. Nick's silver-handled penknife! Gertje was slowly pulling the blade out and pushing it in again, her face intent.

Horrified, Lysbet kept perfectly still and, as she watched, Gertje laid the knife aside, turned in the creaking bunk and thrust her hand under the corner of the mattress. She fumbled a bit and then brought out a wad of blue and white linen cloth, a kerchief she had worn on her head at the orphanage in Amsterdam. She unrolled it carefully and spread it on her lap.

Lysbet could not see all that was in it but Gertje picked up one object, turned it this way and that admiringly. It was a chain of golden beads! Lysbet had never seen them before, but she was certain they did not belong to Gertje.

The girl fondled the beautiful chain, held it about her neck, pressed it to her cheek, caressingly. At length she grew tired, wrapped the beads, the knife and other things in the old kerchief and shoved the bundle under the mattress. She stretched out in her bunk with a grunt of weariness.

Lysbet waited till Gertje's breathing grew regular before she drew back into her own bed. She was aghast.

This was not guesswork. She had seen Nick use his knife to mend his pen that same afternoon. They had both run off at the sight of Judith, leaving the lap-desk and all its fittings in the summerhouse. Here was Gertje with the penknife.

Gertje had stolen it and there was no doubt in Lysbet's mind as to what she must do. At whatever cost to herself, she would go to Mevrouw in the morning. If Gertje retaliated with the tale of the Judges, it could not be helped. She knew they were in safe hiding, their trail forgotten. The thought of Cornelis and his unnamed friends gave her pause. It altered her plan but did not change it. She would confess her crime without waiting for Gertje and contrive to keep Cornelis' name out of it. She could say honestly she did not know what happened that night.

Queerly enough, now that the dreaded thing was upon her, she felt a measure of relief. She did not know how serious her crime was, "aiding and abetting public enemy," or what the penalty might be. She thought she could bear anything if only they did not send her off to Governor Winthrop and the English colony. That awful possibility wellnigh shook her resolve.

She passed a dreadful night, while Gertje, all unconscious of what was ahead, slumbered peacefully.

CHAPTER TWELVE

Gertje

🌷

IT FOLLOWED THAT LYSBET OVERSLEPT HERSELF AND most of the household were astir when she and Gertje, who was always late, pattered downstairs. Lysbet had planned to go first to the garden for the desk but Nick had forestalled her. He had fetched in the desk, discovered and proclaimed his loss. He was very angry for he was proud of his prize knife.

He accused Abram as the most likely culprit, but Abram had been from home the whole afternoon. From school he had gone with the Stuyvesant boys to the Damen swamps after bullfrogs. They were late getting back and the Landt Poort was shut. He complained that the old gaps and broken places in the Waal had been mended and that sentries with guns were walking about everywhere. They had to wait till after dark to get in.

Then it must be Suusje, Nick declared. She had been hanging around the garden all the time he was writing the letter. Suusje denied it with tears and Mynheer Varleth, who was looking up the morning chapter in the big Bible, paused to defend his darling. Nick had no right to accuse anyone without some evidence. He deserved to lose his things if he left them lying about so carelessly.

Judith sat quietly by, all the merriment of last night gone from her face. Almost she wished herself back at Bohemia Manor where nothing ever happened.

Lysbet hesitated. Should she accuse Gertje now, before them all, and clear Suusje? She wanted Mevrouw Varleth to be there, and the Mevrouw was still abed. She had a cold and wanted her breakfast sent up. Lysbet snatched the opportunity, though she felt wretchedly mean as she made the tray ready, while Gertje ran back and forth carrying the smoking platters of fried fish. If she had the least warning of what Lysbet knew she would flash up the back-stairs and hide those things in another place. You must not accuse without evidence, Mynheer Varleth had said. I must do it now, Lysbet thought.

Nick and Suusje were still wrangling as she came through with the tray. Whatever happens this will always seem my home, she thought, as she slowly went upstairs.

"Come in," called Mevrouw Varleth, answering her timid knock. "Is it you, Lysbet? I thought I heard Suusje crying. What is wrong?"

"May I talk with you a little, Mevrouw?" Lysbet stammered.

"Of course, but first put down the tray and hand me my dressing jacket. It is chilly this morning. Now what do you want to talk about?"

"Mevrouw," Lysbet started, "I—I have done something dreadful, a crime, I think—"

Mevrouw Varleth looked at her astounded. "A crime, Lysbet? How could you commit a crime?"

Lysbet started again. "You remember, Mevrouw, when the Lord Director was hunting for the English judges, the regicides, he called them, who were hiding here?"

"I remember there was talk at one time, unfounded tales. Nick told us of them. What have they to do with you?"

"They were here and when Nick told us of the search, I warned them."

"You warned them!" Mevrouw Varleth was serious enough now.

Lysbet told it all, all but Cornelis' name. The Mevrouw did not press her. "I am afraid this must be taken before my brother," she said at last. "But tell me, Lysbet, why do you come with this story today, so long after?"

Lysbet hesitated, but she must speak. "Because of something that happened last night, Mevrouw. I will tell you. It was Gertje's brother and Joris Klenck that stole Mynheer Varleth's gun and the shot and powder too. Gertje knew and helped them. She left that cellar ventilator open for them on Saint Martin's Eve. I knew but I had no proof, and then Gertje found out about the judges. Joris overheard me talking and told her, and she threatened to go with the story to the Director. It was not all for myself that I was afraid," Lysbet pleaded unhappily. "There were so many others concerned."

"I believe you," Mevrouw agreed grimly. "Big-mouth Nick among them."

Lysbet gasped. Not once had she thought of Nick. Of course he was to blame for blabbing. His mother would not shield him, so the Director would be very angry at him too. She had not thought to get him into trouble.

She must go on about Gertje. Her voice flat and wooden, told of last night, of Nick's precious knife, and then the beads.

"Gold beads?" exclaimed Mevrouw Varleth, glancing quickly at the red lacquered jewel box on her table.

"Gold beads," Lysbet repeated. "Not yours, nor Suusje's. I had never seen them before."

"I must get up at once," said the Mevrouw. "Go now and fetch Gertje to me, quickly."

The summons and the look on Lysbet's face alarmed Gertje. "If ye tells anything on me, yer knows what I'll do," she whispered fiercely.

"I have told her already, about me and about you. I saw what you have hidden in your bed."

Gertje stared at her, mouth agape. A cunning look crept into her eyes. "Lem me put on my cap. My hair's a bird's nest." She started for the backstairs.

"No," cried Lysbet, guessing her purpose. "Mevrouw is waiting." Gertje began to run, Lysbet after her.

Mevrouw Varleth was coming down the hall as they reached the top of the stair. She marched past them, up the second flight and flung open the door of their room.

It was in disorder, just as they had left it. Mevrouw Varleth jerked the covering from Gertje's bunk, and the mattress. Bits of broken straw fluttered out. There was nothing on the bare planks of the bunk.

"But I saw her—" Lysbet sprang forward and felt in the corners. There was no crack or opening, no hiding place. She turned to meet the Mevrouw's perplexed face. "I saw her put it there," Lysbet repeated desperately.

"Could you have dreamed it?" Mevrouw Varleth was picking up one of the coverings.

The mattress lay on the floor. Lysbet's foot was upon it. Under her soft house-shoe was something hard. She pounced upon it.

"Wait! Wait! It is inside the mattress!"

Then Gertje leaped at her. "Liar," she shouted. "Was ye put it there." She struck furiously at Lysbet, who staggered back and fell against the edge of the bunk. Gertje was on top of her, fighting like a mad thing. Years of pent-up jealousy broke loose.

Mevrouw Varleth dragged her back, calling for help. Mynheer Varleth had gone to his warehouse but the uproar quickly brought the rest of the family to the scene. They crowded into the little room, Nick and Abram in the front, old Wan in the rear, puffing from the stairs.

Gertje's rage had subsided into gulping sobs. She stood passive while Mevrouw Varleth found the slit in the bed-tick and bringing the blue kerchief from its hiding place, unwrapped and spread its contents before them all. Nick's knife, three odd silver buttons, a little pair of shoe-buckles, trifles mislaid and forgotten, and the chain of golden beads.

"Where did you get this, Gertje?" Mevrouw demanded. "It is none of ours."

"I found it," mumbled Gertje. "I didn't steal any of 'em. I found 'em."

Mevrouw Varleth ignored this.

Judith had followed the others upstairs but hesitated at the door, shrinking from the unpleasant scene. It was Suusje who had come to Lysbet's side to sympathize and exclaim over her bruised temple. As Mevrouw Varleth turned the beads about in her hand, Judith came forward.

"The beads are mine," she said. "My father's gift. I missed them when I was here before. I did not like to speak about it. I hoped, that is I thought, I had left them in Hartford."

"I am glad that is cleared up," said Mevrouw Varleth. "I did not know where it might have led us. Here, take them and be more careful in future. And now all of you go about your business. Later on Gertje and I will visit our magistrates, and see what they have to say to her."

"Lysbet is worse 'en me," Gertje began, but the Mevrouw cut her short. "I know about Lysbet," she said. "That is no concern of yours."

The Court was sitting that morning, and Mevrouw Varleth, forgetting her cold, marched Gertje off. She was kind as well as wise and it was Nick's knife instead of Judith's valuable beads that figured in the charge against her. The court, after lengthy deliberations, with reference to ponderous folios of the "Statutes and Customs of Amsterdam," appointed Mevrouw Varleth, together with her neighbor, Mevrouw Kerstedt, and Domine Megapolensis as arbitrators to decide the girl's punishment. There was no question of her guilt. She was walked away to be kept under lock and key in one of the upper rooms of the Stadt Huys while the arbitrators debated.

Lysbet passed a miserable morning. Her head ached from the bruise on her temple but that was nothing compared to the coming interview. With sinking heart she remembered the mood his Excellency had been in the day before.

Judith hung about the kitchen, her dainty sleeve ruffles turned back. Seemingly she wanted to help. Lysbet was scouring the pewter with sand and ashes. She moved over to make room for Judith.

"I am sorry for anyone in prison." Judith spoke seriously. "I know what it is like. In Hartford while I waited for my brother to come I was wretched."

"But you had done nothing wrong," Lysbet argued. "That must have helped."

"It was being locked in that I minded," said Judith. "Do you think Gertje's brother will come?"

"Hans?" Lysbet shook her head. "He is in it deeper than she is."

Judith was silent for a space, then she said hesitatingly, "I heard what Gertje said— I do not know what you have done but I cannot believe it is very bad."

Lysbet choked a little. "It is not stealing or anything like that, but deceitful and—and—disloyal after they had been so kind to me, and yet I had to do it." Judith asked no more questions.

Late that afternoon Mevrouw Varleth told Lysbet to get ready to go with her to the Director. She said to put on her best beaver-trimmed jacket that had been her Saint Nicholas gift the year before. Lysbet parted her hair and drew it low to hide the bruise.

Mynheer Varleth went with them. His wife had given him in a few words an idea of the affair. He agreed that her brother must be told. Knowing his uncertain temper, neither of them could say how he might regard this flaunting of his authority. Lysbet walked between them, her chin up, her cheeks blazing, inwardly sick with apprehension.

Too short was the distance between the houses; too quickly did Ahasuerus answer their knock; and all too soon she was standing before the Director and Mevrouw Varleth was saying, "Now, Lysbet, tell your story exactly as you told it to me."

Once again Lysbet told it, how she and Abram had lost their way, how she had come to the small bouwerie and had gone in alone and seen the two Englishmen; how the next day she had heard about the fugitive judges, the regicides, and had guessed the connection; how she wished to save them.

"I was sure they would be caught and put to death. They were such kind gentlemen, I could not let it happen, so I— It was late and Mynheer Varleth had said to stay within the Waal, so I—"

"You sent someone to warn them," prompted Mevrouw Varleth.

"Yes, I sent someone to warn them," Lysbet repeated gratefully. "That is all, except that at the cattle market last year, a sheep drover from Connecticut told me that the judges had reached a safe hiding-place far from Niew Netherland."

The Director listened without interruption. His sister and brother-in-law, who knew his face well, guessed before Lysbet was half done that he was not angry, but even they were unprepared for the hearty burst of laughter that followed Lysbet's last words.

"This is the best bit of news I have heard in a dog's age," he said, slapping his hand on the table. "Whatever disobliges Winthrop or Endicott, or both of them, obliges me! I hope the gentlemen judges live long enough to see the son's head follow his father's."

Lysbet was speechless. It was so unexpected. The Varleths were staring too.

The Director retracted hastily. "Perhaps I do not mean all of that," he said, "but I am driven past bearing by their twistings and turnings. When you have leisure,

Varleth, I have a letter here concerning the child that I would show you. Preposterous claims." He glanced at Lysbet and changed the subject.

"You must see this pamphlet new come from London. A vicious document! Nick has had a go at it and unless his English is far astray, it is the grossest insult to our poor Patria that ever was penned. I shall ask Thomas Hall or some other open-minded Englishman to go over it with me. Until then I withhold judgment. Colossal insolence!"

The Director rose and chucked Lysbet's chin. "No more bag o'bones," he said. "I do not ask who gave you that information or who carried your warning in the night, but tell them both that every flea-bite on Winthrop's tough hide pleases me." The interview was over.

Lysbet managed a curtsy and a "thank you, Mynheer," and then before she knew they were on the way home. Mynheer Varleth was the first to speak. "My congratulations, Lysbet. I think it was that pamphlet that got you off. His Excellency might have made it very disagreeable."

"My brother is a just man in the main," said Mevrouw Varleth. "He needs to be managed, that is all. But Lysbet, answer me one question. Was it because those men were English that you risked so much for them?"

"English?" repeated Lysbet, surprised. "No, Mevrouw, that had nothing to do with it. It was the beheading. It would have been so horrible. Almost I would have warned Governor Winthrop himself to have saved him from that."

"Well said, Lysbet." Mynheer Varleth spoke up, "only do not let the Director hear that. He might be hard to manage."

Mevrouw Varleth had to smile. "Run ahead, Lysbet, and tell Wan to make apple-fritters for supper."

Lysbet ran on winged feet. She burst into the kitchen, radiant with her good news. The Director was not angry and all was well. Judith and Suusje, who had been laying the supper table in dismal silence, welcomed her joyfully. Nick played a squawking salute on his flageolet until Judith covered her ears and Suusje flung the board cloth she was folding over his head, effectively silencing him. Abram rushed to her assistance and they quickly had Nick tied up like a batter-pudding.

The tussle was still on as Lysbet danced into the back kitchen to tell Wan about the fritters. A man was sitting dejectedly on the bench near the door. He got up as Lysbet came in and she saw it was Jon Goosen.

He came into the market with his chickens at times and Gertje had mentioned him. He wished to speak to Lysbet now. "I heard in town about Gertje—" He paused and swallowed, "I know you must hate me, Lysbet, an' Gert says as ya don't like her neither, but seein' as we have no friend to go to, I thought mebbe you'd speak to the Mevrouw for me—"

His voice had a humble, pleading tone that touched Lysbet. "She will be here in a moment. It is better that you talk to her yourself."

"She'd not list to me but you, she would. Tell her Gert an' me was aiming to marry, soon as her time was up an' I'd scratched pence enough to pay Domine, an' now comes this! 'Taint as if I hadn't warned her. Times I've said to her, when her'd smuggled me a hunk o' food, 'Gert,' I'd say, 'sometime you'll get caught up with an then who's to help you?' But Lys, you help us now. Beg Mervouw not to be too hard on her."

There had been the stir of arrival. "Come," said Lysbet, catching Jon by the sleeve and dragging him to the door. "Mevrouw, here is Jon Goosen. He wants to talk to you about Gertje. Shall I bring him in?"

"I will come there," said Mevrouw Varleth. "What next?" she wondered.

The interview was long but to the purpose. The Mevrouw recounted it all to her husband later that evening. She had found the uncouth Goosen a better man than she had expected. She had told him the full extent of Gertje's wrongdoing, but he stood ready to marry her if it could be arranged.

"He promises to keep her straight," said Mevrouw Varleth, smiling a bit. "He says there is naught worth stealing in Bergen anyway. I have decided to keep the girl locked up on bread and water, give her a thorough good scolding, tell her she is banished from Niew Amsterdam for a year. Then when she is properly frightened, Goosen, the knight errant, will step in, marry her and carry her off to his chicken bouwerie and keep her there. I have no doubt she will turn out a decent respectable housewife."

Mynheer Varleth began to laugh. "What about your arbitrators—Mevrouw Kerstedt and the Domine?"

The Mevrouw looked astonished. "Why, they will agree with me, of course. What better arrangement could be made? That reminds me, I must speak to the Domine and have the banns cried next Lord's day."

CHAPTER THIRTEEN

Schoolmaster's Wedding

❦

IN THE FIRST FLUSH OF RELIEF LYSBET HAD THOUGHT she could never be unhappy again, but she found two things to mar her perfect world. The first was Gertje. She had been the prime mover in getting the girl disgraced. With her own slate clean, Lysbet began to feel a sympathy for the less fortunate Gertje, languishing in the Stadt Huys. Jon's woeful face had cut her. She had paid him back tenfold for his plaguing at Wiltwyck. All her hatred had gone. She was only sorry.

At church on Sunday, she with the rest of the congregation, was startled to hear among other ordinary notices that Jon Goosen of Bergen and Gertje Kolp of Niew Amsterdam published their intention of getting married. A quiver of surprise enlivened the solemn congregation. Lysbet stole a look at Mevrouw Varleth's impassive face. She has done this for Gertje, Lysbet thought; she is so kind.

That led straight to her other trouble. Dazed as she had been that afternoon in the Director's study, still her ear had caught some words, not meant for her, that carried a threat to her peace of mind: "a letter concerning the child. Preposterous claim!" Did it mean that the thing she had long dreaded had happened at last? Had unknown kinsfolk been found who claimed her, who would take her away from the home and the people she loved?

Day by day she waited for the blow to fall. Nothing was said to her of the letter and she dared not ask.

The obnoxious pamphlet was discussed freely, and it was all the Director had said of it. A mass of untruths, it stated that the expeditions of Henry Hudson had been instigated and equipped by English merchants, and that Hudson had traitorously sold his maps and information to the Dutch; that the Dutch were responsible for dumping the English settlers on a barren country since called Plymouth. Further, that these monsters and usurpers had fraudulently seized the rich Hudson River valley, with its wealth in furs for themselves and finally, that the Dutch in Niew Netherland, as well as the English dwelling among them, would make no dispute about surrendering the Province, if they were once assured of the safe enjoyment of their lands and relief from their unheard-of taxes.

Small wonder that the Director was furious. This outrageous pamphlet had been widely circulated in England. It was anonymous but it was easy to guess the authors: George Baxter, resentful over the forfeiture of his property in Niew Amsterdam, Sam Maverick, a clever

New Englander who had gone back when the King returned and John Scott, after his own advancement. All had been in London at the time and any of them was capable of the libelous document.

Immediately upon learning that Winthrop had returned to Hartford, his Excellency dispatched a formal embassy to wait upon him and his Council to settle certain long disputed questions, Hartford treaty first and foremost. Three leading citizens made up the embassy, Secretary Van Ruyven, Olif Van Cortlandt, and a sensible Englishman, John Lawrence. The Director always dealt fairly with the English of his Province.

As before, his overtures were met with evasions. As to the Hartford treaty, the Connecticut Council agreed "only so far as said treaty conformed to his Majesty's charter." What was Connecticut now stretched south to Virginia and westward to the second ocean.

"Where then is Niew Netherland?" demanded Van Ruyven, angrily.

Truly they knew not, the Councillors replied, unless they could show a patent from his Majesty. His Excellency's embassy returned to Niew Amsterdam, dumfounded.

As the days and weeks rolled by and nothing was said about that letter, Lysbet grew easy. She was happy as she had never been before. Her guilty secret was of the past. In place of the dour Gertje, there was Judith, working beside her, giving her a friendship she longed for.

Judith had lost her mother when she was young and her sisters had married. "My father brought me up," she confided to Lysbet, "and he cared more about Latin syntax than housewifery. I want to learn the nice Dutch ways to please my mother-in-law when I marry."

"For that you could not have a better teacher than

Mevrouw Varleth," said Lysbet, laughing. Judith laughed, too, coloring. Neither of them had forgotten the little scene at the wharf.

Sometimes the two girls sang together as they polished the brass and copper or waxed the fine furniture. Judith taught Lysbet the old Dutch songs, the love songs, martial songs that Dutchmen had sung down the ages as they marched to war. "Our people never bowed to Caesar's legions," Judith boasted proudly. A lullaby, a nursery song, miraculously awoke memories long dormant in Lysbet's heart. Bit by bit the English words came back. She and Judith sang that.

They sang in the long evenings around the fire. Abram and Suusje joining in while Nick played his flageolet.

There promised to be a gay winter. The Esopus war was still a menace but deep snow held the savages quiet. In the spring Captain Cregier would end it with an aggressive campaign, a mighty push. Meanwhile it was simpler and cheaper to send the young men home. The Burgher Guard returned to Niew Amsterdam and were welcomed as heroes.

There were parties and merrymaking everywhere, at the Lockermans, the Van Cortlandts, the Stuyvesants, Van Der Veens, Varleths. Old Klump, the fiddler, was torn from his Vrouw and fireside to play for the dancing.

Lysbet was younger than most of the girls but never lacked for partners. There was always Balthazer Stuyve-

sant, shy and wanting none of the other girls, sulkily waiting for her.

The Lockerman sisters were gay as ever. There was
speculation as to which couple would be calling the
Domine first, Marritje and Balthazer Bayard or Jannetje and Hans Kerstedt. Judith and Lysbet thought it
would be Balthazer and Annetje argued for her brother.

Cornelis Jansen was back at the glass works again,
taller and broader than before. Handsome and sure of
himself, half the girls in Niew Amsterdam turned to
look and sigh after him.

Lysbet took an early opportunity to tell him of her interview with the Director. They were dancing at the Van
Der Veens and had stepped outside with Judith and Nick
to cool off and see the autumn moon rising. Cornelis
said that he had often wondered at her not asking him
questions. It had not seemed quite human, somehow.

"I was afraid of knowing too much," Lysbet said, "but
I would like to know now—"

They sat along the sea-wall watching the moonlight
on the water, while Cornelis described how he brought
the two fugitives down in the night by an old Indian
trail across the island, by the boggy paths of Damen's
wasteland and in through a gap in the Waal, along the
dirty Sloot back of Lockermans and so at last to Berger
Jorisson's smithy.

Before daybreak he and Jorisson had taken the two
judges over to Long Island, up Canapaukah Creek to

Jorisson's mill. There they had lain hidden some few days. Eventually they vanished, Cornelis did not say when or how, except that Jorisson's little sloop made many unnoticed trips, trading up the North River, and along the coasts of Connecticut and Long Island.

"That is the end of my tale," Cornelis finished. "They were fine men, and I hope they are never caught."

"How did they come here?" Judith questioned, "and why did you and Berger help them?"

"What do you know about Berger Jorisson?" Cornelis asked her.

"Nothing, except that he is a blacksmith and that Augustine Heermans says he is a master-craftsman."

"He is that," said Cornelis, "and more, an artist! He has taught me all the finest things I know—to appreciate things, I mean." He broke off. The others stared, only Lysbet thought she understood. She remembered how tenderly he had handled Mynheer Van Der Veen's goblet.

Cornelis went on. "Berger came from Silesia and from simple people, like most of us. When he was about fifteen war ravaged his country and his parents, his brothers and sisters all perished. Friends helped him to escape, and he arrived in Sweden alive but without a stiver in his pocket. Strangers helped him then. He has told me of it often. For their sake he has never turned his back to anyone in need, so when Nelson, the Englishman on Bossen Bouwerie, came asking help, Berger was ready."

"But you, Cornelis?" Lysbet asked. "How came you in it?"

"Oh, I would do most anything Berger asked me to. Besides, I like an adventure."

It was neither Balthazer nor Hans who first called the Domine but Ægidius Luyck, newly appointed Master of the Latin School. The too lenient Alexander Curtius had finally given up and gone home and Ægidius was put in his place. The bride was a pretty young widow, Tryntje Van Vorst, one of the enormous Kip connection.

Schoolmaster Ægidius had no blood kin in Niew Netherland, but his patron, Director Stuyvesant stood by him and opened his house for the groom's supper. In all the festivities the Stuyvesants, the Varleths and the Backers held their ground against the overpowering Kip family.

Judith, Lysbet and Suusje had new dresses, made at the Kip Tailoring Establishment, at a special rate for the occasion.

The couple were to set up housekeeping in the upper floor of the Latin School, one of a row of the small houses facing the Marcktveld. For a week before the wedding the bridesmaids were busy with pails of soapy water, mops and brooms, scouring it from garret to cellar. The neighbors took a lively interest, and the last day Suusje reported with satisfaction that curtains were up in the front windows. The house was ready.

The Stuyvesant supper was on the eve of the wedding, and Mevrouw Stuyvesant provided a bountiful feast. There were speeches, healths drunk, Domine Selyns, from Breuckelen parish, read a flowery nuptial ode which he had written himself. Nicholas and Balthazer Stuyvesant were convulsed to hear their hawkeyed tutor described as a "golden-haired lover."

They danced late, long after tap-toe. The Director himself was dancing, pegging it right and left in great good-humor. Some of the small fry wished that Peter Tonneman, the Schout-fiscal, would come rapping at the door, and arrest both Lord Director and Schoolmaster. That would have been something.

The next day came the wedding. The Domine made it long. Starting from Adam and Eve he delivered an impressive discourse. Later on Lysbet found she could remember none of it. Could she have been asleep?

"You could and you were," Judith giggled. "I thought you were resting for the bride's party tonight. I tried napping myself but Domine kept lecturing poor Tryntje on being an obedient wife. It was enough to make her change her mind and run before it was too late."

Fast on the heels of the wedding gayeties came trouble. John Scott appeared on Long Island with a couple of hundred ruffians at his back. He marched about haranguing the people, altering the good Dutch names,

Middleburgh to Newton, Amersfoort to Flatlands, inciting rebellion. One rumor said Winthrop had sent him; another was that he acted for King Charles, and still another report said that he was there on his own account. In whichever case, he and his unruly followers were presently engaged on a career of plunder. They seized the block-house at Niew Utrecht, crossed the island in a stride, occupied Breuckelen and menaced Niew Amsterdam across the narrow East River.

Reports of all this were brought to the Director, who was furious. The city was practically unprotected. Many of the young men of the Burgher Guard were in town but they were unorganized. Captain Cregier and the experienced troops were miles away in Wiltwyck. The Director posted a lookout on the roof of the tall Stadt Huys to watch for any aggressive move.

It was not long in coming. A flat-bottomed cattle-barge crowded with men, put out from the Long Island shore. It looked like the start of an attack.

The Director summoned whom he could, Secretary Van Ruyven, the Domine, and the Schout-fiscal, Peter Tonneman. They were despatched in haste to meet the invaders and "talk sense into them." Meanwhile the Director scraped about for any man or boy who might be found.

Schoolmaster Luyck, peering from his class-room window, saw the need and dismissed school for the day. He and all the older boys were supplied with muskets,

powder and shot from the fort, and started on a run for
the ferry-landing.

Director Stuyvesant had an added cause for anxiety.
His big bouwerie was only a mile from the ferry-landing. If Scott and his rabble were after plunder, the road
was open to them. To make things worse Mevrouw
Stuyvesant was there. After the wedding she had gone
for a rest and to make all snug for the coming winter.
She had called it a holiday and invited Judith, Lysbet
and Suusje to go with her. They had lingered, enjoying
the crisp autumn weather.

The final day came. In the afternoon Lysbet suggested
a last walk. They might visit the knoll where the chest-
nut trees stood and gather some nuts to take home.
Judith was lazy and would not go, so Lysbet and Suusje
set off by themselves. Job, the sheep dog, joined the
expedition. They followed the path to the water, running and shouting like little children. They reached the
chestnuts but there were no nuts. These were gone to the
squirrels, or to the riffraff from the fishermen's huts by
the ferry-landing.

Taking a trail that followed the water they ran along.
They might find other nuts or better still, bright autumn
berries. They went for quite a distance then came out
on a rocky point, from there they could see all around,
the woods and marshes, the low hills of Long Island.
Half way across the water was a cattle-barge, slowly
propelled by oars. It was crowded with men, not cattle,

and a flag flew from the short mast in her bow. It was too far away to distinguish but to Lysbet it seemed strange. She strained her eyes as the scow drew nearer. It was not the Dutch flag. The color was wrong. At last she saw clearly, white, red and blue. The standard of England! What did that mean? Under the very nose of Niew Amsterdam! Lysbet and Suusje stared at each other.

"Let us go," Lysbet said. "We can pick up the ferry trail at the end of the marshes." They ran, Job in the lead, barking madly.

Still another party was converging on the ferry-landing. Abram Varleth, Nicholas Stuyvesant and young Martin Cregier had found the afternoon too beautiful to stay in school. They had gone after hickory nuts. Armed with short boomerang clubs to bring down the high fruit, they had gathered a great store from the trees on Bouwerie Road. They were passing the point where the ferry trail met the road when they were startled by the sound of gunshots. Not from the wilderness to the north, as might be expected, but from behind them to the East. As one boy they turned and made for the ferry trail.

Half way along they caught up with Lysbet and Suusje, hesitating. The firing came from the landing, they said. There was a cattle-barge, filled with men and flying the English flag. Suddenly there came more shots.

"Come on," shouted Martin Cregier. "What are we waiting for?" He started pellmell down the trail, the others close behind him. They burst out of the woods at the landing. There lay the barge. The men, some thirty or more rough-looking fellows, had come ashore. They lounged about, waving their guns, firing now and again into the air, to intimidate a stolid little group of fishermen and laborers from the huddle of shacks near the landing.

In the midst of it all, the renowned Captain Scott strutted about, issuing orders and dire threats. The flag which had so dismayed Lysbet, floated from an old Maypole which between whiles did duty as a flagstaff.

Lysbet and Abram pulled up short, yanking at Suusje. The others crowded in. Martin, a born fighter, pushed in front.

"Haul down that flag," he shouted.

Scott whirled on him. "What's that? Uncover, you young ruffian. Take off your hat, I tell you!"

Far from taking off his hat, Martin brandished his club and spat contemptuously. Scott pounced upon him, wrested the boomerang from his hand and began clubbing the boy over the head and shoulders.

Abram and Nicholas rushed to Martin's aid, dragging at Scott's arms and coat-tails. Job leaped into the fray and grabbed him by one leg. A blind rage swept over Lysbet. Above the shouting of the others, the half-hearted cheer from Scott's men, she heard her own voice, clear and loud. "Stop it, you brute! Stop it, you brute!" over and over in English.

It is doubtful if Scott even heard her, though he did glance in her direction, over her head and beyond to the shore line. What he saw there gave him pause. Mynheer Van Ruyven, Domine Megapolensis and Peter Tonneman marched abreast and behind them came Schoolmaster Luyck and his eager scholars, brandishing their weapons, a few added recruits.

At this display of power, friend and foe alike took to their heels, the spectators to their shanties, the invaders to the barge. Scott shook himself free of the boys and dog and stood his ground, but only for a moment, for one glance informed him he was alone. Step by step he retreated towards the barge.

"What is the meaning of this?" demanded the Domine, loudly.

Scott did not answer but as he reached the edge of the landing, he turned. "I go now," he shouted in bad Dutch, "but I will return."

"Return!" Secretary Van Ruyven shouted back. "This is Dutch land, and we will give you a Dutch welcome, fine fellow."

"I will stick my rapier in the guts of any man who says this is not the King's land." With that Scott jumped down onto the barge, calling to his men to push off.

As the gap widened between the barge and the landings, he shouted again. "And when this place is King's land, ye will have more freedom." With this finishing shot the valiant Captain Scott departed.

The defenders were left triumphant but with their number suddenly depleted. Martin, dazed from the beating he had got, stood alone. Lysbet and Suusje were at one side, holding Job by his shaggy coat. Nicholas and Abram had disappeared as if by magic.

Meanwhile Schoolmaster Luyck had yanked down the flag. He stepped over to Martin.

"Martin," he began solemnly. "You see what happens to boys who play hooky. Let this be a lesson to you. If the Domine and Mynheer Van Ruyven agree with me, you may keep this flag as a reminder. You practically captured it single-handed."

"Oh, no," Martin protested modestly. "The others—"

"Others?" exclaimed Ægidius, a twinkle in his eye. "Were there others? Well, tell them from me, that sooner or later, their sins will find them out."

CHAPTER FOURTEEN

Hans and Joris

❦

THE ACTIVITIES OF HANS AND JORIS WERE ATTRACTING
attention.

Late in February Mynheer Varleth had word that they
had been seen hanging about Jock's Tavern. Peter Tonneman, the Schout-fiscal, went after them, but they had
disappeared. It was said that they were on their way to
do business with the upstart, Scott, who was continuing
his evil doings on Long Island.

For John Scott had broken a written agreement, which
he had given his followers and had put Dutchmen off
their land, claiming that they had no title to it. The five
Dutch towns pleaded that without help they must find
themselves under his domination or else Winthrop's.
That gentleman was swearing vengence on his own account, threatening to prick John Scott's bubble.

Nicholas Stuyvesant stopped in at the Varleths' and
said his father was so upset there was no living with him.

"I am not surprised," said Mynheer Varleth, "considering that our few Company men are at Esopus and no
immediate help is in sight."

"And the doubt that our fine Company will ever send us enough help," said his wife.

Mynheer Varleth shrugged his shoulders. "If they are not madmen, they will. Winthrop may settle Scott's pretentions in time, but then we shall have him on our necks. He knows our weakness full well."

"Father says we must play for time," said Nicholas, then went to Abram to ask help in a mathematical problem.

The rest were clustered about the fire. Mynheer Varleth and Petrus at the chessboard, Mevrouw knitting a long red stocking, Lysbet fondling Mi-mi, the kitten, Judith playing cat's cradle with Nick. Suusje had gone home from school with Katryntje. It was time she was home, Mevrouw Varleth said, for it was getting dark.

Dropping Mi-mi Lysbet jumped to her feet. "If you please, Mevrouw, I will go for her."

There had been a three days' thaw. The piled-up winter's snow was melting fast. The gutter in the center of Marcktveld was a running stream. Lysbet was glad of the light from the White Horse Tavern at the corner of Brower Street. That was also afloat.

Mevrouw Van Cortlandt lent them a lantern for the way home. They paddled along, Suusje sliding, then splashing the puddles. She clawed snow from one of the banks and threw it wildly.

Lysbet laughed in derision. "I bet you a beaver that I

can do better." Shifting the lantern she formed a hard, well-shaped ball and aimed it at the tavern's swinging sign.

Suusje gave a hoot for at the same instant one of the customers stepped out of the tavern. This ball, also missing its mark, hit him square on the cheek. The man turned quickly. The girls saw a bearded face, eyes that glinted with anger.

Lysbet jumped forward stammering in dismay, then saw that it was Dirck Goosen. He knew her too and his ugly scowl changed to a sickly grin.

"A sweet welcome from an old friend," he mumbled.

Suusje was laughing and Lysbet gave her a warning look. "I did not mean to strike you, Dirck—I tried to hit the sign—"

"You owe me many, since Wiltwyck days," said Dirck, evidently trying to be agreeable. At any rate 't was a lucky meeting being as I were on my way to see ye."

"To see me?" asked Lysbet, thinking that she would prefer never to see or think of Dirck again.

"Leastwise, Collector Varleth," said Dirck. "I got business wi'he."

They walked in silence past Jansen's the baker, Johannes De Paistre, then the Latin School. Suusje had stopped laughing. Lysbet held the lantern to guide their steps. "How is Gertje?" she said at last.

"Oh, she be well enough," said Dirck, "but think me she were raised too soft. She wants this en' she wants that. Mor'n poor men like me an' Jon can afford."

"She should be glad that she is not in jail," Suusje piped up.

"Ye's right there," said Dirck, emphatically, "an' but for Jon she would ha'been, as I tells her every day."

They had passed Mynheer Steenwyck's store now and were striding a roaring torrent in the gutter. What can Dirck want with Mynheer Varleth? Lysbet thought. What business could there be between them? She wondered if it were Gertje.

Suusje, who loved to tell news, ran into the house first. "Dirck Goosen is here! Lysbet hit him with a snow-ball."

"What are you talking about?" Mevrouw Varleth exclaimed.

"Straight on the cheek," gasped Suusje, doubling up with mirth.

"Dirck Goosen! What does he want?" Mynheer Varleth pushed aside the board irritably, for he had just seen a move to corner Pieter's king.

Lysbet, with Dirck back of her, had just appeared at the door. It concerns you, Commissioner Varleth," Dirck shouted over her shoulder. "But first I want to get this clear. In cases of smuggling, like, how much do the man who puts ye into the way of seizing the goods get as his share?"

Mynheer Varleth glanced at him sharply. "One third of its value."

Dirck pushed Lysbet aside. "It's this," he said, striding into the room. "Will ye pledge your word to play fair wi'me?"

"Tell me what you are after," said Varleth. "If you have something to tell me of a smuggling operation and it is of value, certainly you will be paid at the fixed rate."

Dirck looked about uneasily. " 'Tis for your ear only, Commissioner."

Mynheer Varleth stepped into the entry crowding Dirck before him. "Stop your quibbling and get down to what you have to tell me." He shut the door.

Lysbet and Suusje took off their cloaks and hoods and came to the fire.

"Can you guess what the lout has in his mind, Lysbet?" asked Nick, curiously.

As he spoke a sudden suspicion struck her. Gertje's demands for more and more. Hans and Joris. There was no chance for them to sell their furs in Niew Amsterdam.

The outer door slammed and Mynheer Varleth opened the second door. "I will have to return to the Custom Huys," he said, "and Petrus, you go to the fort and tell them to collect the crew of the revenue boat. Tell them to report at the wharf."

Mevrouw Varleth laid down her knitting and rose to her feet. "Is it Hans and Joris, Nicholas?"

"Yes," said Mynheer Varleth. "They came with a great load of pelts a couple of days ago. Have been with Jon and Gertje. They left Bergen this morning to hide in one of our marshes, and will cross to the Long Island tonight. Much as I dislike this way of getting the information I will have to use it."

"I would strike this fellow with a fist rather than a snowball," said Nick. "Though Hans and Joris are rogues."

"We can leave him to Gertje," said his step-father. "If we catch the pair she will ask Dirck where he was that night. He will not tell her but she will guess."

Mevrouw Varleth went with him to the entry, wound a thick scarf about his neck, helped him with his cloak. "I do not like you standing about that cold wharf. It is all so unpleasant."

Nick, meanwhile, was bundling into his own outdoor garments, evidently aching to take an active part in the affair. He went off with Petrus and Mynheer Varleth.

Balthazer had been at the Lockermans' but came home for supper. He said that he had seen a light in the Custom Huys, and going in had talked to his step-father. The revenue boat had started out and Burger Jorisson, happening by, had joined the hunt in his sloop.

"Where are Petrus and Nick?" asked his mother.

"Oh, are they not here?" said Balthazer, with an over-innocent glance about the room.

"I suppose that means that they are on one of those boats," said Mevrouw Varleth, knitting on her stocking furiously. She laid it down. "Well, we must get our supper over with. Then you can take some to your father and perhaps build up his fire."

By common consent no one went to bed. Suusje curled herself on one of the settles and dozed. Judith and Lysbet took over the chessboard. Abram, yawning from time to time, wandered about aimlessly. Mevrouw Varleth sat with the hour-glass at her side, and with her needles clicking. The tenth hour, the eleventh, the twelfth, passed.

It was after midnight when her husband and sons came in. Mynheer Varleth sat down by the fire to warm up, and Balthazer pulled off his boots.

"I was surprised to see the light," he said. "You should all have gone to bed."

"We were anxious," said his wife, letting her hand drop to his shoulder.

Reaching up he took it in his. "Well, Anneken, we got what we were after and more besides. It was not only the duties on the pelts that we might have worried about.

"These rogues had evidently been back and forth. They had a letter from someone up the river to Scott. It told him how we are involved at Esopus, and of our weakness here. It said that there were those who would rise up and help him take Niew Amsterdam whenever he said the word. There might have been a pretty mess if it had been delivered."

"It is horrible to think of such traitors amongst us," said Balthazer, angrily. "What can we do?"

"Keep our eyes open," Nick broke in, "and we have a plenty of stout fellows that can do that. It was Cornelis Jansen, on Burger's sloop, who spied them on the hinter side of Nooten Island. He was at the helm and without a peep to any of us, swung about to and cut them off. Old Burger saw them then and said, 'Get your guns ready. Just in case—' I had no gun so I took the helm. There was a wind. They did not have a chance—"

"Yes?" said Abram, his eyes like saucers.

"Just as we came up to them, Hans jumped overboard. Cornelis dropped his gun and went after him. It was nip and tuck with them both for the current was strong and the water icy. Hans was swept away (we will have no more worries with him) but Cornelis, seeing that Hans was gone, by some supereffort bucked the tide and caught hold of our boat. Then we hauled him in."

"And Joris?" Judith exclaimed. "What became of Joris?"

"The revenue boat had come up by then and got him," said Mynheer Varleth. "They found the letter and took the furs, a pretty catch. The varlet is in jail now. Will doubtless be sent to the Indies. He is an older man than Hans, a hopeless traitor and criminal."

"Poor Hans," said Mevrouw Varleth, "and poor Gertje. This will be a terrific blow to her."

They gave the Director the letter in the morning. He called a meeting of his council. Although disaffection had been suspected here and there, this was positive proof. They decided that it was of supreme importance to protect Niew Amsterdam, the key to all Niew Netherland.

It was not for them to dispute whether their land belonged to the Netherlands or King of England, was under the protection of their High Mightinesses or of the Company. Their duty was to resist all attacks on their property and liberty, burghers and townsmen within the walls, the Company's soldiers outside.

The next day there was a notice in French, English and Dutch posted on the Stadt Huys. The Lord General and his Council wished to borrow 27,000 guilders for the defence of Niew Amsterdam. This should be paid in five years in wampum, the interest at ten per cent.

Tongues wagged, for this was a measure forbidden by the Company. But his Excellency's name headed the list, then the City Council, the Deaconry of the Church, Domine Megapolensis. The loan was oversubscribed.

News arrived in March which changed but did not brighten the situation. Governor Winthrop had sent troops who had arrested Scott and taken over on Long Island in the name of Connecticut. To make matters even more disturbing it was said that King Charles had given this same Long Island to his brother, the Duke of York.

Director Stuyvesant sent letters to all the towns of Niew Netherland. There would be another convention in early April at the Stadt Huys. He wrote again to the Company, sending this letter on a Van Rensselaer ship. If there was no immediate settlement between the King and States General, the Company must send instant and sufficient reinforcements in men and ships. Otherwise he and his people could not be held responsible for what might ensue. They had not yet obtained even the single man-of-war that they had long ago demanded.

The convention met in early April. Representing the oldest colony in the Province handsome Jeremias Van Rensselaer presided. Mynheer Backer was one of the two delegates from Niew Amsterdam. His wife reported to her sister, Mevrouw Varleth, that each town thought of its own meager defence and none of Niew Amsterdam's. There was general anger at the Company. Petrus had told them that he had done all he could, and they themselves, too little.

In the middle of all this turmoil Balthazer elected to speak for Marritje.

His mother was vexed at such bad timing. "Who feels like a wedding just now?" she asked him.

"Obviously Balthazer," said Nick laughing, "and Marritje—"

"I feel like a wedding," said Suusje, "I always feel like a wedding."

Looking at Judith, Nick felt like a wedding himself, but did not think it tactful to mention it.

Lighting a candle Mevrouw Varleth went to the fore-room, all the young people trailing after her. She unlocked a chest in which she kept her most precious possessions. It had come from France with the Bayards, then from quiet Alphen, to sail across the ocean.

With intent eyes upon her she took out a beautiful

ivory fan, a Spanish shawl, lengths of silk, some from the looms of France and Italy, some from the East, prizes, perhaps taken by Dutch privateers in the Spanish wars.

Suusje reached for an end of silk and rubbed it softly against her cheek. "Can Lysbet and I have dresses of these when we are married?"

Opening a lovely sandalwood box Mevrouw Varleth took out a double betrothal ring. One half had been worn by herself, the other by Balthazer's father. His oldest son should wear it now, and give half of it to Marritje. In the bottom of the chest, wrapped so carefully, was Samuel Bayard's wedding suit, black velvet trimmed with silver gimp and buttons. All his sons should wear that at their marriages.

CHAPTER FIFTEEN

Niew Amsterdam Falls

❦

In May the Company sent sixty soldiers, a small supply of ammunition and with them a statement that the States General had ratified the Hartford Treaty. They added that without doubt King Charles would do the same.

Meantime Winthrop was taking over on the Long Island and claiming all of it by right of his charter. His Excellency, with members of his Council, had gone to him, hoping to make terms. Winthrop refused, saying that the Indians who had sold the land to the Dutch were not the rightful owners.

In the midst of the general bewilderment the Lockermans planned an elaborate betrothal party for Marritje and Balthazer. The city rocked with preparations, the guests furbishing up their costumes and searching for gifts; rival bakers buying up all the sugar to make wedding confections, bride's sugar, sugared almonds, and a sweet drink called bride's tears.

A few days before the occasion, ominous word was

brought of an English fleet, under the command of a Colonel Nicolls, which had drawn in at Pascataway.*

Marritje cried as if this were a special spite against her.

Her bridegroom joined others in piling gravel on the walls of the Fort. Although of fine construction, they were but two or three feet thick and in some places only ten feet high. In its present state it could never withstand a heavy bombardment.

While the tension was at its height, a second letter arrived from the Company. Sir George Dowling had assured them that the fleet had sailed on a peaceful mission.

Marritje dried her eyes. The city resumed its usual gay disorder. Ships came and went. One carried an order to Amsterdam for a wedding dress, a crown and cake. The betrothal ceremonies, a nine days' wonder, took place. Marritje stitched on her present to the groom, Govert built them a house. The young couple would start with gold spoons in their mouths.

The Esopus war was ended with a virtual wiping out of that nation. It had been made evident that it must be either they or the Dutch, and the Dutch were stronger. Again peace was signed with the neighboring tribes, this time at Niew Amsterdam.

In the midst of the joy at this happy event a war be-

* Portsmouth.

tween the Mohawks and Mohegans broke out at Fort Orange, the Mohawks threatening English settlers. With a warning to Winthrop the Director started up the river, hoping with his influence to settle the matter.

He had been gone a scarce two weeks when disastrous news was heard. Nicolls, now in Boston, was recruiting men from Massachusetts and Connecticut to attack Niew Amsterdam! Burger Jorrison, whose sloop was the speediest craft in the Province, volunteered to sail up and tell his Excellency.

Dropping all else the Director came home. A day later the *Guiana*, flagship of Colonel Nicolls, swept up the harbour, dropped anchor at Gravesend.

With undaunted courage the Director organized a further strengthening of the Fort, but even with the men from Esopus, its garrison was only a hundred and fifty strong and the hills to the north made it vulnerable. In case of siege the well was without its walls.

To make the situation worse, Niew Amsterdam was dependent on a steady flow of food. Anticipating the harvest a huge cargo had just been shipped to Curaçao.

As Mevrouw Stuyvesant and her household were at the bouwerie the Varleths decided to send the girls there with Abram. All its laborers were in the city, helping with its defence. Balthazer and Nicholas, aided by women and children, a few old men, were trying to gather in a harvest and send it down.

At the last minute the Van Cortlandts and Kerstedts sent Katryntje and Annetje, to add their mite.

The party rode on a cart which had come down loaded. Abram walked with old Ahasuerus kicking up the dust. A tall boy of fourteen, he would rather have fought.

They were quenching their thirst at Fresh Water when they heard a rider approaching. It was Balthazer Stuyvesant, with his mother behind him. Abram rushed up the bank to shout that they were going to the bouwerie.

Balthazer drew in his horse, "They will be glad of your help." Lysbet caught a glimpse of his face. He had never looked so much like his father.

There was a direct cartway to the barns. As they drew near they saw Nicholas in smock and klumps, directing the loading of a second cart. He stood in a golden mist as two old threshers beat at a pile of grain. Four stout women, their petticoats tucked up, were taking his orders.

"The Lord General of the petticoat detachment," Judith yelled. "And here are five recruits, a captain in command."

Nicholas turned, wiping the sweat from his face and neck. "Tuck up," he laughed, "We will put you to work."

"Picking peaches and such like," said Judith, "so we can eat too."

"Ump," sniffed Nicholas, "and Niew Amsterdam starves!" Walking over to help the children climb down, he added, "What is the news? Mother was frantic. She and Balthazer bolted, leaving me here."

Abram spoke up. "They say more ships have come, war-ships and transports. They know our waters for they have been used to come here. Uncle Petrus would welcome them now with powder and shot, but his hands are tied."

"Tied indeed," said Nicholas furiously. "If disaster comes the Company deserves it—"

When the cart drove off they all went to the fields. The scythes felt heavy to Nicholas and Abram, but the women, strong as men, cut swich, swich across the length of golden wheat, then back again. The children followed to straighten and bind up the sheaves and the girls joined them, working till their arms ached.

Balthazer did not return but Ahasuerus and one of the old men went back and forth pretty constantly as the carts were loaded. They reported that Domine had gone to Nicolls to demand his purpose, Director thinking it best to send a man of peace, but Nicolls had said 'twas to take Niew Amsterdam, just like that, bold. Director says, don't ye believe them. England and Patria is friends, they is, they've just signed a pact. Nicolls would never fire.

Nicholas rode to town on the next load. When he returned his report was not so encouraging. There was a large fleet of three war-ships, innumerable smaller vessels and transports. They had taken a hastily constructed blockhouse on Staten Island and were blockading the Narrows, patroling the river, shutting off most of the food supply. Nicolls had sent a letter saying that if the city surrendered, it should not be harmed. His father had not published the contents of this letter. Some were so fearful they might favor surrender.

Lysbet drew in her breath. "I hope that we never surrender."

Judith glanced at her in surprise. "That sounds strange from you, Lysbet."

Lysbet's face crimsoned. She was unhappy all that evening and the next day.

Judith saw that something was wrong. "I did not mean to hurt you, Lysbet," she said at last. "It would be only natural to like your own people best."

"But it is not like that," said Lysbet, eagerly. "There are some who are your own people by blood, and then there are other people who are yours by love." After hesitating a moment she told Judith of little Beaver. "He gave his life for me. That is what I mean."

"I understand!" Impulsive Judith threw her arms about Lysbet's neck.

It seemed even more important that they should send all they could gather to town. Nicholas had some of them digging potatoes, others shucking Indian corn. The children went into the orchards and skinned the trees. It was a relief from the everlasting binding. Esther handled the milk, for the Director had an enormous herd of cows. They made butter, packed and sent it with the buttermilk.

Nicholas went again with this load. He was angry at Balthazer for not returning. They were all frantic for news.

"The Council has forced Father to publish Nicolls'

terms," he said shortly, on his return. "There are some who would accept them but Father will not."

At supper he told them more. A delegation headed by Winthrop had come with a white flag to the city wharf. They had met with his father, the Council and Burgomasters. After hot words Winthrop had gone, leaving a letter. "Director Stuyvesant," he begged, "you should not provoke a needless war when peace, liberty and protection are intended. Resistance will only mean a willful protraction of the inevitable end."

"What impudence!" exclaimed Abram. "I trust that Uncle Petrus tore it up."

"That was exactly what he did," said Nicholas. Interrupting a cheer, he continued in a less triumphant note. "Someone told, and there was almost a riot with people clamoring to see it. They had to piece it together, bit by bit. Then Nick copied it and put it into French and English."

Judith spoke: "Then what happened?"

"Father still feels that Nicolls will do no more than frighten us with idle threats. I left him writing a letter. As Nicolls knows Dutch he could write it himself. He insists on our rights and says truly that the Hartford treaty must be by this time ratified by their king. He demands that nothing shall be done till we both hear from Europe."

"That will end their pretensions," said Judith.

It was towards evening the next day that Janse, one

of the children, came running to Lysbet. "There is one who would speak to you, jonge juffrouw. Down by the chestnuts."

Letting down her skirts Lysbet cut across the fields. Most everyone was in sight but could Balthazer have come up by the forest trail? Janse's klumps sounded at her heels and she stopped and ordered him back. If Balthazer was in one of his low moods, and she thought it likely, he would not want Janse.

She saw no one at first, but stopped in the shade of the trees, wiping her face, pushing off a lock of hair. It was warm and she had hurried. Could this be an impish trick of Janse, she wondered.

"Let me see your face, jonge juffrouw." The sudden voice behind her made Lysbet jump. Turning quickly she was relieved to find that it was an Englishman whom she had often seen at market. He had a truck garden at Midwout across the East River.

He knew her, too, and taking a letter out of a pocket handed it to her. "It is writ in English. Can you read it?"

"I think so," said Lysbet. It was not addressed but on fine paper, sealed with a great splash of wax, an S made by a signet ring. She turned it curiously, then tore it open. The first words, "My dear niece Elizabeth," caught her eye.

She glanced quickly at the man, "Who gave you this letter?"

"If you read it then you will know," said the man.

With her heart pounding she laboriously traveled down the page. Some of the words were beyond her but not the sense. It had come at last. And at such a time.

The man was looking interestedly at the house which could be seen between the trees but turned to her as she spoke to him. "Did this gentleman," she glanced at the signature, "Captain Sutherland, come with the English ships?"

"That he did," said the man, with a nod.

"He tells me that you will take me to him," said Lysbet. She was frightened, her heart was as heavy as lead. What did this thing portend?

They followed the river and took the path to the ferry. The forest was dense but there was a break at a small inlet where she and Suusje had often waded. Lysbet realized that it was here that the meeting was to be, for there was a boat drawn up and a tall figure waiting. He must be Captain Sutherland, her father's brother, her uncle. As she approached he leaped up the bank and came to meet her with outstretched hands. His cloak flew back and underneath she saw a soldier's uniform.

Hardly knowing what she was doing she stopped short, scowling at him. Her escort took her by the arm and tried to draw her along.

Her uncle stepped quickly, "No, Smith, do not force her." He added, "I had looked for a warmer welcome, Elizabeth."

"You came with the ships." Lysbet had not expected to say that but the words burst from her.

Captain Sutherland glanced at her sharply. "Yes, for I had heard of this project and asked for a special assignment. There was the possibility of trouble and I did not purpose that you, my brother's daughter, should be exposed to it."

"What makes you think I am your brother's daughter?" asked Lysbet.

"We do not think, we know," said her uncle. "The first clue was an unsigned letter, which said that an English child was living in Niew Amsterdam, that she was of the right age, that she had been ransomed from the Mohawks. We were referred to Arendt Van Corlaer of Rensselaerswyck. We placed the matter in the hands of Governor Endicott who wrote begging Van Corlaer to find out further details from the savages with promise of added ransom. This he did and the date of your capture tallied with the time when my brother and his family were attacked. You had come from a settlement on the Pascataway River. Then there was no doubt."

Lysbet remembered Governor Endicott's letter which had come over a year ago.

"Why did you not tell me before?"

"Because that stubborn Dutchman Stuyvesant made an issue of it. We were told that you were happy and that you were to be given a choice later. But the question of choice is no longer in Director Stuyvesant's hand, or in the Varleths' or yours. This fellow has rowed me over from Flatbush and you must return with us. Arrangements have been made to send you to Boston. I will take you to England later. In the event that my son does not live, you would be the next in succession to our place, Cloomber Hall. I see that you have beauty. You will have money and position also. It will be good for you, my dear."

Lysbet had been biting her lips to keep them from trembling, but she knew now it was her turn to speak. This was her father's brother and he was kind, and he had taken much trouble for her. "I—I do not know how to say it well—but it is a shameful thing that you do— To come here to take Niew Amsterdam. Surely you can see that?"

"Higher powers than I have settled the matter. After all, we must obey the King's will. He agrees that it is not well to have an alien people between his New England and southern colonies. If the Dutch submit peaceably they will not be molested and their property rights will be respected. Never in all history have better terms been offered."

"We will not submit," said Lysbet. "Never."

"Then the city will be taken by force. In addition to trained troops we have New England volunteers, with others under the command of Governor Winthrop."

At the mention of Winthrop Lysbet saw red. "When

you tell me this I think more than ever I will not go
with you. Nothing will make me feel that it is not wrong
what Governor Winthrop does, and your King—"

"You look like your mother," said her uncle, "but
you act like your father in not seeing to your own advantage. He chose to align himself with a set of malcon-
tents who finally got what they sought—stiff-necked
Cromwell, but before it had come to that our father used
his influence to get land here and shipped his troublesome son over."

"And my mother?"

"Your mother loved him, so came with him. As it
turned out, she lost her life for him."

"And I would lose my life for them," said Lysbet, pas-
sionately—"Mevrouw Varleth, Mynheer Varleth, his Excellency, all of them. I am grateful to you for wishing
to help me but if you had not come to threaten us I
should be more grateful."

Her uncle put forward his hand. "I see that you re-
semble your mother in more than your looks, Elizabeth. But I beg you to tell these people what I have told
you. The King wishes to take Niew Amsterdam without
destroying it but take it he will. The Stuarts, for all their
easy ways, are stubborn. We have had means of knowing
how weak its defences are; that is why Nicolls is pa-
tient. There will not be one stone left on another if we
have to bombard. Although Nicolls is a humane and just

man it is not possible to control an invading force. Our soldiers and Winthrop's rabble will finish the destruction."

Lysbet took his offered hand. "I will tell them," she said. "Thank you and I am sorry." Stumbling over roots, catching her dress in brambles, she sped back to the Stuyvesant house. The tears ran like rain down her cheeks. As she got near she saw Balthazer. He had just arrived. Ahasuerus was taking away his horse.

"Oh, Balthazer," she wailed, "I have something so dreadful to tell you—"

Taking the edge of his pocket handkerchief he wiped her face. "Why Lysbet," he said, half laughing, "what could be dreadful enough to make you weep like this?"

"But there is, there is! Just wait till I tell you. Then you must ride to your father and tell him."

A man on his way to Niew Haarlem stopped off the following day. Nicoll's ships had sailed up the harbour, under the very walls of the Fort, and were anchored there, he told them. "It was seen that they had moved all their guns to the city's side, so if we fired, they would open double fire. Lord General stood by our cannon the while, a gunner, with a lit match, beside him. When the ships came to anchor his face looked fearsome, they say. Domine took him by the arm and led him away. As a parting blow he said, 'Nicolls gives us forty-eight hours to surrender.'"

Nicholas broke a horrified silence. "I must go to Father."

"Can I ride behind you?" said Abram.

"I want to go too," said Suusje, "We all want to go—"

Judith, who had looked pretty sober, laughed. "Suusje, it is only boys who get what they want, but remember, boys, come back or we will all pile after you."

They came back before the evening meal. Everybody on the place was to be collected in the house, they said, and the dogs must run and the guns be kept ready. Scott had fled from Hartford and was at Breuckelen with a mob. They could be kept off in force but a few might slip over.

Nicholas had not talked to his father but had seen him on the balcony at the Stadt Huys. There had been a crowd outside demanding he yield and he had shouted louder, telling them he had written again to Nicolls. There had been hoots, greater anger. "Enough of letters!"

Nothing happened that night. The children slept, the women dozed. In the morning Nicholas told them that none should go to the fields. There was a secret place in the cellar and Ahasuerus dug it out. They hid the priceless silver and other valuables, a box of jewelry that Nicholas had brought from town.

Balthazer came that afternoon. The dogs barked an uproarious welcome and the siege was raised as everyone rushed out to meet him. Giving over his horse he stepped up to the stoop. "It is all over," he said bitterly, "We have surrendered."

His face frightened them all. "Come," Lysbet dragged him into the house and to a chair. The others followed. "Then Nicolls refused Father's terms?" Nicholas stammered.

"They were his terms, rather, a white flag at the fort."

"But surely," Lysbet gasped.

"Could you see Father agreeing to that?" said Balthazer. "He sent word that he would die first. But the people did not want to die—Nicholas, Abram, you saw how they were the other day. Now they were even worse. Furious at Father and at the Company."

He turned his face and buried it in his hands. They heard his voice muffled. "We wrote a petition—we begged him not to reject Nicolls' terms—to resist was suicide, absolute ruin."

"We?" said Nicholas. "Who do you mean by we?"

"Nick wrote it. We all signed it. Mine was the second name—" His shoulders were shaking. "Father gave in—he could not stand against even his son—"

Lysbet jumped to his side. "Balthazer! I know it would have been easier not to sign. You had to do it!"

The capitulation was arranged outside the city wall, at the Stuyvesants' bouwerie. There were six delegates on each side, two Englishmen, handsome and courteous, who had come with Nicolls, others from Massachusetts, Winthrop of Connecticut, with his long, dour face.

Mynheer Varleth was there for the Dutch, Oliff Van Cortlandt, Cornelis Steenwyck of the eagle eye, Samuel Megapolensis, son of the Domine, Burgomaster Cousseau, Councillor De Decker.

They made good terms, these Dutchmen. Their garrison should leave with full honors of war. Only English regulars should march in. Scott's men or Winthrop's men were to put no foot on Manhattan.

How Governor Winthrop felt as to the reliability of royal promises no one could guess, but he had only an unwilling New Haven, nothing else for which he had hoped. Long Island, as well as all of Niew Netherland, had been given to James, the Duke of York and Albany, the King's brother and heir.

His Excellency led his soldiers out of Fort Amsterdam, his head proudly erect. Never had he looked more stubborn. The men carried their guns and their colors went before them. They marched to the rap tap of their own drummers. They went to the wharf by way of Beaver Lane, then the Heere Graft, for they would sail immediately for home.

The English soldiers, waiting on the Heere Weg, marched into the empty fort, then raised their flag. Nicolls, Deputy Governor for his Highness, the Duke of York, took possession.

CHAPTER SIXTEEN

Lysbet Sails Again

❧

THE YOUNG PEOPLE RETURNED, THE CITY SETTLED DOWN. It was now New York, the fort, Fort James.

English officials replaced the Dutch, the calendar was changed and the names of the streets. The river was now Hudson; Fort Orange became Albany. The Van Rensselaers and others might keep their large holdings but pay taxes to the Duke.

The Lord General moved up to his bouwerie, which should now be their home. The new Governor Nicolls took possession of the mansion. It was now called Whitehall, after the King's palace in London.

There were some who said that it mattered little if one paid to the Duke instead of to the Company; that it was a fair exchange from their tyrannical Director to the amiable Nicolls. But they were in the minority. Most of the people loved and respected their Lord General as never before. He was a good fighter and a good loser.

Small satisfactions were enjoyed. First, Winthrop's disappointment; then Scott, with his pretensions

squelched, Baxter, who had appeared, claiming all of
his former land. Governor Nicolls made short work of
him. The King had used them all when it pleased him,
then had dropped them.

At the height of all this readjustment and heart burn-
ings, Captain Sutherland called at the Varleths. He had

come upon Elizabeth too suddenly, he said, and at an unfortunate time. It was inconceivable that she should not at least consider his offer.

Lysbet saw him. He was handsome and dignified, but she had not changed her mind. Saying that the matter must be still kept unsettled, he left with some of the ships.

The Varleths, with others, subsided to their usual routine. Though skies fall, folk must eat and drink, sleep and wake. Mynheer Varleth was no longer Commissioner but he had his own affairs. Attractive Nick, speaking English, was shifted to another post. Claiming that this change absolved him from his promise, he clamored to speak to Judith. His mother told him to wait one more year, then she would see.

Marritje's crown and wedding dress arrived and she and Balthazer were married. Nicolls graced the occasion and was most complimentary. It was noted that he and General Stuyvesant, uncle of the groom, talked in a most friendly fashion.

Suusje and Lysbet, with Judith, were bridesmaids and all three had new silk dresses.

Balthazer left home. Petrus went too, unhappy at the changes about him. Returning to his Uncle Heerman's at De-la-warr, he talked of taking up land. Before Petrus sailed Hans Kerstedt, who was working with his father, betrothed Jannetje.

In February a letter arrived from the Company for

their former Director. They had protested the loss of possessions to King Charles with no satisfaction. Would General Stuyvesant return to the Netherlands as they wished a better understanding.

"Pish," said his Excellency. "Understanding! One man-of-war at the Narrows would have kept them their possessions. Even Nicolls says so."

Writing that he would go if a suitable ship was sent, he spent the rest of the winter fuming. Mevrouw Stuyvesant reported that his rage warmed the house. He would take his sons but leave her in charge of the bouwerie. After he gave the West India Company a strong piece of his mind, he would return, live and die there.

The ship, a man-of-war, arrived in May. It would carry General Stuyvesant home.

Shortly before they left, Balthazer rode down to the Varleths on a beautiful horse that his father had given him. He said that he had especially come to see Lysbet. His aunt laughed. "She and Judith are weeding the pansies, but if you wish her for something very special take her to the summer-house."

Balthazer blushed easily. "It is rather special." He looked solemn as he escorted Lysbet to the summer-house. What is the matter now, she thought, stopping to pick one of the yellow daffodils. She held it under his chin then stooped to peer closely. "Oh, I see gold," she laughed. "You will be rich, Balthazer, very, very rich."

He caught her hand. "That is strange, Lysbet, in view of what I have to tell you."

"What have you to tell me?" said Lysbet, pulling her hand away.

"I have been talking to Father. I told him that it is as impossible for me as it is for Petrus to live in Niew Amsterdam, to see that Nicolls about and be pushed aside. I am ashamed even to look Father in the face. He must think me a weakling, not to have stood with him to fight with the last breath in my body." The words had tumbled out but now he stopped and looked at her. "You, Lysbet, may think that too, but truly, it was what your uncle had said. I thought of my mother and you and Suusje and Aunt Annetje and all the rest—"

"Balthazer, I know you were right," said Lysbet. "Perhaps not to give in sometimes is a sort of pride."

Balthazer's face brightened. "Lysbet, Father has offered to give me his plantation at Curaçao. He had always intended it for Nicholas but he would rather stay here. I will go with them to Amsterdam for I want to be at Father's side in case the Company blames him, and also see something of the world. Then I will go to Curaçao and live under Dutch rule as I have always done."

Lysbet was distressed. "Balthazer, must you go so far?"

"It is far to go alone," said Balthazer. "Lysbet, do you think—I love you next to my mother, and of course she would not go. Lysbet, would you marry me if they let you, and go to Curaçao with me?"

Thinking it was a joke, Lysbet looked at him half

laughing, then saw that it was not a joke. "Oh, Baltha-zer," she said, "I—I do not think so—"

"I suppose you do not love me," said the boy, gloom-ily. "After all, I do not see why you should."

"Of course I love you!" Lysbet spoke quickly. "But Balthazer, I am scarcely sixteen and you are the same, not wise and experienced enough to be a husband."

"I suppose you think Cornelis Jansen is—"

"Is what?" asked Lysbet. "And what has he to do with it?"

"He has this to do with it. He likes you too. I saw him looking at you at the wedding."

"Nonsense," said Lysbet. "He was just thinking how much nicer I looked than I did at first. He could get any girl in Niew Amsterdam and you know it."

Balthazer was not satisfied. "Lysbet, Father tells me that Curaçao is beautiful. Our's is a sugar plantation. Life will be easy, not hard as it is here."

"But I like it here," said Lysbet, thinking, "First my uncle, now Balthazer."

"Well," he said, "I will come up often to see my father and mother. Perhaps when I am older you will change your mind."

A couple of days after this interview, Governor Nic-olls called at the Varleths. He presented them with a letter from Lysbet's uncle which had come enclosed in one to him.

Captain Sutherland said that he and his wife were not willing to resign their whole claim to their niece; that she should be given an opportunity to meet her father's family and see English life before she made a just decision. Later in life she might regret that decision, and reproach the Varleths.

They asked that she might come to them for a year and if at the end of that time she wished to return, they would use no compulsion.

"But how could that be?" said Mevrouw Varleth. "We cannot send Lysbet to England as if it were across our Ferry. It is a dangerous voyage and long. We would not allow her to go alone."

"But that can be arranged," said Governor Nicolls. "I am giving sailing permits to your brother and his sons, and also to several Dutch families who are selling their property here and returning to Amsterdam. Elizabeth could sail with them under the protection of your brother and in the care of one of the women. Captain Sutherland would meet her at Amsterdam, take her to England."

"Governor Nicolls, this is something that we cannot decide in a moment," said Mynheer Varleth, firmly. "We must think it over and talk to the child."

It was a grave question. Did they have a right to bind Lysbet to a choice made ignorantly, in a time of stress and anger. No one could tell yet how things would be here, and the offer was tempting. Would Lysbet regret?

Calling her at last, they put the matter before her. Both they and her uncle thought that her final decision should be made with a clearer idea of what it might mean. They suggested that she should go to England for a year, then either stay or return.

Lysbet looked at them startled. "You would wish me to return?"

"We would wish it greatly." Mynheer Varleth spoke gravely. "You are as one of our own children, Lysbet. While Gertje was here we could not make too much difference but you must have known how we felt."

"Oh, I have known," said Lysbet, tears welling to her eyes. "You could not have done more for me."

"You have done more for us," said Mevrouw Varleth. "Suusje's life, for one thing, then the gift of your love."

Lysbet sank to her knees before her. "It was not a gift, Mevrouw. I was almost a savage when you took me. I cannot say it right but it is my payment. I can never pay enough to you and Mynheer Varleth and Suusje and Nick, and all the rest."

Mevrouw Varleth kissed her very tenderly. "Lysbet, we wish you to go to England. We love you and wish you to have all the good that life may give you. If you prefer our simpler ways and will come back, we shall be happy. You will sail with Uncle Petrus. Captain Sutherland will meet you at Amsterdam."

"Amsterdam! Will I see Amsterdam?"

Mynheer Varleth laughed. "Amsterdam and London too. Then come back to Niew Amsterdam."

The city turned out to see them off; red men and white men came from afar. It was a tribute to their Lord General, Silver Peg to some, who for seventeen years had ruled them through storm and stress, sometimes with an iron hand, but always according to his highest duty.

Lysbet, weeping a bit yet smiling too, stood at the edge of the family group, the Varleths, the Backers, the Stuyvesants, now the Lockermans, the Van Cortlandts, the Van Der Veens, tied to them by Balthazer Bayard's marriage.

Mevrouw Stuyvesant, overcome with emotion, held her son Balthazer in her arms. It was bad enough having them all leave her but the others would return.

Balthazer was weeping openly. "I will come up often, often."

The great Dutch ship was anchored off shore. It had sent its landing craft and the oarsmen were at attention. Those on Schreyers Hoek must tear themselves apart and say the last farewells.

Cornelis Jansen, who had been standing with Evert Duyckink and one of his fellow apprentices, a group of the boys, strode from them suddenly and came to Lysbet's side. "Lysbet, have you heard my big news?" he asked.

Lysbet turned quickly. She had wanted to speak to Cornelis but had not known quite how. She had felt shy with him since Balthazer's speech.

"I am sailing too!"

"Sailing?" said Lysbet, hardly believing her ears. But Cornelis was laughing. She had never seen anyone look so utterly happy.

"Evert Duyckink only told me this morning. He and Mevrouw Stuyvesant have cooked it up between them. I am going to Bohemia, to Italy, if I choose, to learn fine glassmaking. It is what I have always longed to do. We can make it here. We have the sand, oceans of it and only lack the skill."

"Then you will come back?" said Lysbet. "It is not forever you go."

"Of course I will come back," said Cornelis. "I love every blade of grass, every stick and stone. This land is good." Then he added a bit doubtfully, "But you, Lysbet? I hear that your people are rich and important. You may not wish to return."

"Oh, I will," said Lysbet. "I love every blade of grass, every stick and stone, just as you do, Cornelis, and I love more besides—I love people."

Cornelis looked at her. "I love people too, but I did not think to say so. All the joy of coming back will be to find them here." He hesitated. "When you come again I shall not be a clumsy apprentice, making window glass or painting fire buckets. When I close my eyes at night I see the things I want to make, lovely forms, beautiful colors. In my dreams I see them."

"I want to see them too," said Lysbet.

Judith and Suusje were pushing their way towards them, Suusje weeping. They had said good-bye to Lysbet, but wished to do so again, then had just heard that Cornelis was going. "Good-bye, Cornelis, good-bye and good luck." Suusje threw herself in Lysbet's arms.

As the anchor was weighed, the sails lifted, the Dutch crowded to the city side. Things had changed and some were glad to go, others were regretful.

The Honorable Petrus Stuyvesant, largest landowner on Manhattan, no longer hampered by the Company's lack of judgment, went because he would go. He went to give the West India Company, possibly their High Mightinesses, a piece of his mind, tell them what he thought of their stupidity, then he would return, do his part as a law-abiding, loyal citizen.

Lysbet, Cornelis and his sons drew close to his side as a salvo from the fort rang out and the English flag dipped. He swept off his plumed hat, but the tears coursed down his weathered cheeks.

With tears on her own cheeks Lysbet thought: First was the land, good as Cornelis said. The Indian loved it but did not know enough to keep it. Next came the Company and they only wanted to take from it—they did not love it. The English King? Well, he does not love it either.

She looked at Uncle Petrus. Here was the answer. It is men like him, like Mynheer Varleth, like Cornelis, even Governor Winthrop, who love it and work for it and live on it who should possess it. It came to her with a flash. Perhaps if we do not see it, our children will. The English flag may not always fly here.

The End